WORDS AND WOMEN:

ONE

2014

CAMEO

First published in 2014
By Unthank Cameo,
an imprint of Unthank Books
www.unthankbooks.com

Printed in England by Lightning Source, Milton Keynes

A CIP record for this book is available from the British Library

Any resemblance to persons fictional or real who are living, dead or
undead is purely coincidental.

ISBN 978-1-910061-01-5

Edited by Lynne Bryan and Belona Greenwood

Cover design by Rachael Carver

CONTENTS
WORDS AND WOMEN: ONE

Introduction:

Questions you may ask, answers we will give.

– The Editors –

Why women-only?

Why not? Anthologies generally have a focus: greatest young writers from Ireland, thirty stories about cats, best flash fiction of all time…

Less flippantly, this anthology arises out of the work of Words And Women, an organisation which started as a small reading event held in Norwich, Norfolk, to celebrate International Women's Day in 2011. The event was fun and interesting, and was so well-received that it refused to be a one-off.

Now Words And Women continues to celebrate International Women's Day but also offers women writers in the East of England other opportunities to present their work and to talk about writing. Organisations like Vida (www.vidaweb.org) actively explore the critical reception of women's writing today and provide a vital forum for debating inequality and imbalance (it continues to exist); Words And Women chooses to place most of its energies and resources into simply providing a platform for voices which it feels need to be heard.

Why these writers?

The anthology features the work of 21 writers who entered Words And Women's first writing competition which was launched in July 2013. The competition was open to women over the age of 16 living in the East of England. It was for prose work – either fiction, memoir or creative non-fiction – under 3,000 words in length. We received very many entries and selected the very best to appear here, including Dani Redd's wonderful short story *My Sister's Haircut* which won first prize.

Is there anything else we should know?

• Words And Women have had a few women ask why their work wasn't selected for the anthology. All entries to the competition were judged anonymously and what caused one piece of work to stand out from another was a combination of great style, an awareness of form and shape, and interesting content. Interesting content became the deciding factor as we looked to build an anthology which would be varied, would have a balance of fiction and non, and would introduce readers to new worlds and experiences.

• The writers included in this anthology have worked on their pieces with the editors but the writers had the final say over everything but the most basic layout. This means there are differences in the way pieces have been punctuated for instance, the dialogue in some pieces is signalled by speech marks but not in others.

Who would you like to thank?

Unthank Books for its support and Ashley Stokes, in particular, for his help and invaluable advice; Rachael Carver for the marvellous cover design and Rose Cowan for providing the papercuts for the cover and for Words And Women's distinctive logo; Vicki Johnson for designing the competition posters; Guinevere Glasford-Brown for running Words And Women's Twitter account @ wordsandwomen; every funding body that has given a grant and every woman who has given their time to help out Words And Women; and a big thanks too to all of you who entered the competition.

Happy reading!
Lynne Bryan and Belona Greenwood,
February 2014

Wellfleet

- Lily Meyer -

We sat cross-legged, knees touching. The sand was hot on the bare backs of my thighs. Della had recently given up shaving, and the hairs on her shins glittered with salt. Rosie was crying behind her sunglasses. "It's stupid. She's never going to give a fuck."

"Her loss," I said. Della hummed in agreement.

"She told me she's still in love with Lucas."

Della shook her head. "Lucas's still in love with me. And he's a douchebag."

"Fuck Lucas." Rosie's voice snagged. "He's awful. Carmen told me he never makes her come after they have sex. If she doesn't come before he does, fuck it. He just falls asleep."

"He was the same with me. I used to do it myself half the time. He never even watched."

"She told me I give the greatest head. You know what she said once? She said if she could be all the way gay she would, just for me, but she can't." Rosie pushed her aviators onto the top of her head and wiped her eyes with the inside of her wrist. As she replaced the glasses she took a long, shuddering breath. "No more fucking straight girls. I'm done."

A seagull circled us, cawing, then flapped away towards the dunes. I wrapped an arm around Rosie. "I thought Carmen was bi."

"Bi-curious," Rosie said miserably. She dropped her head onto my shoulder.

"Do you love her?" I asked.

"No. I think so." She sighed. "Yes."

"That counts for something."

"Not if she doesn't love me."

"Sure it does," Della said. "Every time you love someone it stretches you out inside."

Rosie snorted. I burst out laughing, and Della joined in, rolling her eyes. "Okay, not like that. Like you learn how to do it better. How to love better."

"How to fuck better," I continued. "Well, not for you."

"You know what, someday when Tony and I have sex, it's going to be great."

Rosie sat up. "When's that going to be, on your wedding night?"

"Or if I ever convince him the Virgin Mary doesn't care if we bang."

"You actually think you might marry him?" I asked.

"I think anything that ends in us fucking."

"Go back to what you were saying before," Rosie said. "How love stretches you out like a vagina."

Della tossed sand at her. "So when I started dating Lucas freshman year, I didn't know shit."

"That's why you were dating Lucas," I told her. "That and the free weed."

"Didn't hurt. But I'd never had a boyfriend before in my life. It was just, oh my God, this hot guy wants to have sex with me and he wants to talk to me? We must be in love. But we never gave each other anything, which as it turned out was because Lucas is a hideously selfish individual."

Rosie interrupted, "What do you mean, you never gave each other anything?"

"Like, he talked all the time about what happened in his head, his worldview, all of that. He wanted me to get him. And I did, I always understood what he was talking about, and it seemed like we had this amazing connection, and I loved him for it. But I never talked. I only responded. Half the time it seemed like Lucas was talking to himself and I just happened to be there. When I broke up with him I remember thinking, The next guy I'm with, I want him to understand what's in my head, too. And Tony does."

"You're just saying that being in relationships makes you better at relationships," Rosie said.

I dug my fingers in the sand. "I don't think that's true. I think I'm worse at relationships than I used to be."

"Well, you're nuts," Della said. "You used to be normal and now you're insane."

"True." I tilted my head back and looked at the saturated blue sky.

"Not that I should talk, given that I've been with Tony for nine months and I've never seen his penis. I know I'm crazy for doing this."

"Oh, I'm crazier than you," I told her. "You know how long I'd been with Gabe before I told him I loved him? Not that I'm with Gabe."

"Yes, you are."

"Gabe isn't my boyfriend. Gabe and I are not officially exclusive. For all I know he's fucked every hooker in Thailand by now."

"While emailing you every five seconds about how much he loves you?" Rosie said. "Shut up."

"I'm just saying, he could have. Anyway. The first time I told Gabe I loved him was the sixth time we slept together."

They stared. Waves crashed on the sand. "The sixth time?" Rosie echoed.

"Yep. And this is me and Gabe, right, so the sixth time was literally the sixth day. As in, the first time we had sex was a Wednesday, so this was the Tuesday."

"You know it was a Wednesday?"

"It was a Wednesday."

"Wow." Della held out her hand for a high-five. "You are crazier than me."

"You know how we decided to go to Mexico together?"

Rosie pushed her sunglasses up again. "I forget."

"It was three weeks before graduation. Gabe was over, and we'd just had sex and we were talking about our, you know, our thing. How great it is, and how much we were going to miss each other, and he just said, I can't say goodbye to you in three weeks. I can't do it. And I said, me neither, and so we got on Expedia and Kayak and — what's that one? — Student Universe, and we looked to see where we could both afford to fly, and it was Mexico, so we bought tickets."

"That's nuts." Rosie was smiling now. "That's so romantic it's disgusting."

"That's not disgusting. It was disgusting when we both got the shits from eating fried cactus at a street cart in Mexico City."

A wave licked close to us, leaving streamers of seaweed. "Tide's coming in," Della said. "We should go swimming."

I looked down the beach. Umbrellas fluttered in the distance, candy-striped and tipped to the sun. There were no clouds in the sky, no figures approaching. "We should go skinny-dipping."

Della bounced to her feet. She held out her hands, hauled Rosie and me to our feet, saying, "Last one out of her suit's a rotten egg!"

I laughed, tugging at the knot of my bikini top. "You're such a fucking camp counselor." We ducked out of our halters, shimmied our bottoms off, left them piled on the sand like burst water balloons. We lined up giggling, linked hands, counted to three, and then ran.

The ocean was cold on my feet, cold up my thighs and on my belly. Rosie dropped my hand as I plunged underwater. I popped back up and grabbed, dragging her with me.

"Motherfuck – !" she spluttered. "It's freezing!"

I splashed her. "Welcome to the East Coast, bitch." Her boobs floated pale as moons below the surface. I looked down at mine, made out the blue veins running up from my nipples. "The water's so clear today."

Della swam toward us, her neck arched high. "Why is swimming so much better when you're naked?"

"'Cause your tits float," Rosie said instantly.

"They float anyway."

"No, they feel floatier without a bathing suit," I agreed. "That's definitely part of it."

"And it's less cold somehow." Rosie was squinting toward the horizon. "What's on the other side?"

"I think Portugal," Della said, standing. The water lapped at her shoulders.

"Isn't Portugal warmer than here, though?"

"Maybe not in the north bit. I don't know anything about

Portugal."

"It's amazing how much we don't know," I said. "Don't you think? We just graduated from college. I thought when I graduated from college I would have read more, I'd have more ideas about how the world works, but I don't know shit. I'm completely clueless. When I was in Mexico I kept thinking, here I am in this country directly south of mine, this country whose language I speak more or less fluently, and I don't know anything about it. I don't know Mexican history, politics, literature, nothing."

I kicked onto my back and floated, the sun stamping white circles across my vision. My mouth was full of salt. Rosie was saying, "Maybe that's why I keep being such an idiot with Carmen. I don't know anything yet."

"That's part of what I meant," Della responded. "Obviously Carmen isn't as horrible as Lucas, she's not a drug dealer or a complete egomaniac – "

"You think Lucas is an egomaniac?" Rosie said. "I kind of think he's a sociopath. Aren't they supposed to be super charming?"

"He might be. The point is, Carmen's not comparable to Lucas, but she's been jerking you around for months, and that's never really happened to you before, right?"

"No, it hasn't."

"So maybe next time you'll know better, or you'll be able to protect yourself, theoretically."

"But then how does that fit with the more-room-for-love thing?" I asked, still floating. "Because I think that's true. Two years ago I don't think I was capable of loving anyone as much as I love Gabe."

I let my legs drop to the soft ocean floor. Rosie was drifting next to me, eyes closed. "How much is that?"

"I love him so much I could choke. It feels like I'm going to puke half the time, or like my ribcage is going to explode. I can feel how much I love him in my finger bones."

Rosie opened her eyes and pushed herself vertical. We were standing in a triangle now, just our heads above water, slick as seals. Every wave forced me onto my toes. "You make it sound awful."

"It's a good thing." I felt water trickling down my forehead, into the hollow next to my right eye. "It's painful."

Della spat into the ocean. "What isn't? It's painful for me that Tony and I have this huge gulf between us, that he believes in God and I can't, and that might wreck our relationship, but I still love him. And meanwhile Lucas goes around hurting people and saying it's because he loves me, and that's painful, too."

"Well, it's painful for me that Carmen goes around not calling me back for weeks and saying it's because she was with Lucas and then still expecting us to fuck. And it's painful for me that I do it."

"But next time." The seawater was nipping at my eye now, inside the corner. Gabe was eight thousand miles away. I didn't believe myself as I said, "Next time we'll know what to do."

"Or the time after that."

"Someday," Della said. I squeezed my eyes shut. They felt dry under my lids, but when I opened them water streamed out and the salt sting was gone. Through my wet lashes the ocean shimmered pine green. Della was facing the horizon, but Rosie was watching me. There was a black ringlet flattened against her cheekbone. I reached out and pushed it behind her ear. She touched my hand as a wave rolled by, and we drifted together in the current. Her mouth was softer than I expected. She held onto the small of my back, our knees and stomachs brushing together as we kissed.

When it was done I saw Della looking at us, blushing. She smiled and flicked a bit of water our way. Rosie and I watched her for a second, and then I dove underwater, swam to her, came up and kissed her. She tipped her head and sucked at my lower lip, her eyes closed. Rosie was swimming toward us already. Della and I bumped noses, laughed as we lifted our faces apart. Rosie surfaced and we held our hands out to her, linked arms again, and the three of us splashed up to the beach, naked and dripping, together.

The Call

- Caroline Jackson -

Queenie Bird's funeral was traffic news in the local rag. Traveller Standstill Tomorrow! How was that for ironic? Of course, they were missing the point because what was primarily interesting was the fact of the occasion, not its appeal to public curiosity, though that had its importance. Such convocations were remarkably rare, and equally problematic, for the reasons she'd explained. Without question, there'd be others also thinking along the same lines. Nonetheless, there could well be a footnote or even a short paper to be had out of it.

That had been Luce's departing salvo when Thomas came in from choir practice. She'd already eaten with the children so they were done, just Hannah's times tables to hear, up and down, after recorder practice, before Isaac's soya, then bed, no later than eight. Helmet on, and off she went, just in time to catch the start of the planning meeting, bicycle straining under its armour of recently redundant baby seats, rear- and crossbar-mounted, lights and laptop-heavy panniers stuffed with knowledge. Thomas, his head cocked under the low lintel, watched her weave away like a well-packed camel confronting the desert.

As told, stir-fry didn't really keep hot very well though the optimum temperature for digestive efficiency was, apparently, within one or two degrees of the body's own. So that made it much more palatable. Thomas's appetite had, in any event, lost its edge in contemplation of the next day and its approaching flood of possibilities. A plateful of slippery, drooping noodles that demanded nothing more than mastication as he ran through his address was, in its solitary and still colourful way, quite comforting.

Peers from theological college had seemed impressed when they heard. Most were in team ministry, leading their ragged and tenacious congregations in harness with others, believing themselves part of a purposeful caravan, knowing others to be in reach but, too often, feeling blinded by a stinging sandstorm of indifference. When, from curacy, Thomas Avery was to his admitted surprise, and quiet astonishment, appointed Rector in Charge of All Saints, Cheynham, a thirteenth-century beauty crouched, as if grazing, on the fen-lapped side of the city, it was no surprise, none at all and not before time, to Dr Lucy Stokes, Junior Research Fellow at Christ's, mother of two and vicar's wife designate; in no particular order. Her post doc on the correlation and synergies between the application of new technologies (expand) and homeopathy in the controlled settlement (perceived?) of migrant Inuit colonies in Northern Labrador should, finally, complete during Thomas's probable five-year tenure. Rest assured.

Following their respective doctorates, Luce had fully understood, actually endorsed, the selection panel's advice that Thomas should seek some real life experience before committing to his vocation but, as those initial two years teaching history to restive schoolboys in a smaller, less cerebral, university town had doubled and stretched, so had the distance between their hopes and fears. In his mind's eye, Thomas still saw in her small, terrier face and perpetual motion, the fragile confidence and eagerness he'd fallen in love with on arrival as a fellow postgraduate. She'd been, still was, enchantingly real after hours adrift with the metaphysical. Had she time to linger in the mirror, Lucy might also still have recognised it, albeit now paper-thin and camouflaged by commitments, clean teeth, good nails and a quick brush of mascara. Her few, tentative, grey hairs at either temple were the only external indicators that zest had given place to zeal with neither declaration nor admission.

She had, however, never lost faith that he would make it. Now she was right, and loved him for it. They had arrived, in what was, to those in the know, a marked parish, one for those on the up, on their way. It was invigorating.

Blessed with a rare, barrel-vaulted, azure-washed ceiling, supported by bosses of chalky, hot-cheeked plaster angels, All Saints had been built many centuries ago for scholars of the new university. It was noted in various estimable, if arcane, architectural authorities as one of the few acknowledged traveller churches, favoured by the itinerant community. So not just an ecumenical oddity but a cultural oxymoron, and note the lower case! For Thomas, it was no hardship to return to where they'd met in what sometimes felt like another life. He'd been freshly garlanded with a first degree from the Other Place, she bolstered by a local First in Anthropology, both now set on something higher. The ancient city had been a kind crucible for their love and his new-forged faith. He and Luce could never forget those idly industrious, shared years of study. They'd been novices in an idyll that tethered them together. He'd enjoy rediscovering it with her, and the children, putting down roots. All Saints welcomed its new incumbent with a service of dedication, thirty per cent of the funds for a new church boiler already raised, open invitations to speak at Cheynham's Women's Institute, Scout troop and retirement home and a vestigial choir in need of harmony.

Even though their current behaviour, at the challenging end of the spectrum, was proving hard to reconcile with the optimal two and half-year interval in their ages, Thomas had faith that their children would, too, soon settle. Lucy wanted to eliminate all possible deficiencies, mineral or social, to which Hannah's and Isaac's wild outbursts and feral fighting could be attributed. A pigeon pair, at each other's throats, he suggested they just didn't really like each other. It seemed pretty normal. Healthy was a word he avoided.

They moved into a vivid Elizabethan rectory, held up by dog roses and shaped by its shadows. It made slight noises day and night as if it had just arrived and was still settling or was preparing to depart unnoticed. Adjacent to the moss-silenced, nest-filled churchyard, the house appeared to have grown from the ground like a huge, fleshy fungus, keeping its counsel as to whether it stood friend or foe, unlike one of the Commissioners' recent acquisitions, all double-glazing and flimsy partition walls, porous to confidence. Luce needed no encouragement, convinced of their title and endearingly purposeful. Everything would soon be under control. Thomas found himself imagining the space it would create when it eventually crumbled away.

"You'll say a few words, Father, though don't be worrying if there's not many listening. They'll be thinking of her going on, devout as she was, and the Big Man won't bother about any canting. So go at a lick, 'cos we'll all be needing a good slug."

Dandy Bird, Queenie's eldest son and head man since the passing of his father, Daniel senior, whenever it was, Blackthorn winter, that time when the freeze kept 'til May, best skating for years, eight of his own and all of thirty-five, stood on the doorstep, up close to Thomas as if staking a claim. He wore a Tattersall shirt and waxed country jacket, both of which looked new. A day or two's growth clung, tidily, to his squire-shaped chin. He wouldn't come in, could they speak outside. He looked very solid and it wasn't a question. No music but his people would want bells. A peal. Six for a woman. None of them would forget how good the priest had been, visiting the site; his girl said he was a doctor too, read it on the hoarding, up by the church.

Behind her father's shoulder stood the daughter, too tall for herself, as if height had stolen a march on hips, a punter's pick, coming up the outside. Her dark chestnut hair was long and compellingly straight, groomed to a polish and contained in a band. Oxford blue eyes looked at him, unknowable, from her flat, milky face, high-cheeked and capped with a strong widow's peak. A teenage Mary Stuart in a sheeny tracksuit, she smelt faintly of Luce's nail-polish remover, like a really ripe pear. Thomas was peripherally aware of a large, iridescent car waiting beyond the gate.

When they'd gone, Thomas knew he'd been party to a deal to which he was neither coerced nor reluctant, merely passive, like a tree shaken by a passing squall. Dandy Bird had extorted from him his mother's ticket and Thomas was complicit in the transfer. What troubled him as, from an upstairs window, he watched them drive away was a feeling that the daughter, whose name he hadn't heard or perhaps it hadn't been used, would like to have been involved in the service, could have read a poem or said a prayer. If she were allowed. He'd noticed her scanning his shelves.

Downstairs again, Thomas saw through his study window a green-faced tabby lope, solitary, through the overgrown border that spread across the end of the garden. It wove among the marguerites which had, all this first summer, stood their showy ground, surrounding the inherited cultivars which seemed to bloom only for each other, polite and futile, among the weeds. The cat matched precisely the between-tides colours of the children's climbing apparatus, a miracle of freecycling, built from sustainable wood seasoned to a virtuous shade of lentil, which floated on the neglected lawn. The feline visitor left no trace. Eulogising Mrs Bird daunted him, not because he presumed anyone would be listening, but because she seemed to have, still, a presence in troublingly inverse proportion to her reality. As if all the smoke generated by the ceremonial burning of each and every one of her possessions in the days after her death, something he'd witnessed and about which he'd found himself mediating with the powers that be, had seeped via the downdraught of her departure into his world. Perhaps if you left more, many more, offspring than the years you'd lived, you were transformed into permanence, a sort of eternal folk memory beyond written record. Beyond anything he might offer. If all sixty of her grandchildren were to appear at the funeral he could extrapolate a gathering of Biblical proportion. Its simple presence should give meaning to his words. Thomas caught himself, mute, looking back from the glass. Why, then, did he know that his funeral address would be like a tribesman's lone arrow, spinning up vainglorious and desperate from the forest floor, scattering its frail feathers at the huge metal monster passing far overhead?

During her last days, he'd been to her scrubbed caravan, not Mr Toad's gaudy fantasy, but a convincing, pearly motorhome. Rings of children, peeled off the air, had surrounded him like a celestial convoy, Old Testament faces perched incongruously on their slogan-togged bodies, heads cocked, legs braced over tough little bikes. Their intent interest had clamped on him like a change in atmospheric pressure. He'd felt them waiting outside Mrs Bird's, as he gave consolation among the arrangements of sturdy, synthetic flowers and over-coloured pictures of Jesus. On his final visit she'd been breathless and gasping, unable to see him out. She was not old when she died.

Thomas's notes, all questions, slipped from his desk in a strewn-straw mess when his study door swung open. Expecting Luce back, he saw instead the girl standing there, her velour tracksuit, cardinal red, flattened by low light to the colour of clay. A matching swan-necked girl stood beside her, touching. He noticed that their big, silvery hoop earrings swung in synchronicity. Both had what must be their Christian names branded across their chests in sparkling swirls. Once, as a small boy, he had been hurried past the fortune-teller's hutch on some east coast pier, rushing towards the grey horizon to reach the knockabout justice of Mr Punch, that poor Baby and the great, greedy crocodile at the end of the line. Feet dragging, he'd glimpsed a different trinity that now stole back into his head like the sound of a cuckoo. Hoops and hands and a chenille tablecloth, not unlike his parents' candlewick bedspread, but smoother and darker and more promising.

"Maria and me think you should know more about her." Dorothy's words were quick and sticky-sounding, seeming to bubble out from the back of her long neck as she looked round the room. Maria, to rhyme with liar and fire. After such sudden apparition, why was he surprised when she spoke? And spire and higher. She said think, not tink. Were they the graceful heralds to a scam, the men casing the joint as they held him captive? It gave him a thrill of sorts, though brushed with disappointment, that there was nothing they could want from his domain; the accoutrements of a practical life, tools and materials and suchlike, didn't figure large in the Avery household though Luce had been making inroads. Dorothy continued, her words sounding cussed in the bookish sanctuary. "Queenie Bird had the caul so she knew when she'd go. She told us. So don't be upsetting the children. Please, the little ones, they're mad to see the horses, black with pink plumes and all them flowers. She's gone, left nothing, so we can go on now."

The strange logic made perfect sense to Thomas, occupying him for the few minutes after they'd left until he saw the gap. An empty space, hip height, at the end of the top shelf of the bookcase which ran along the wall, flush to the open study door. The Collected Poems of George Herbert, his working edition, gone.

Luce, returned, had had no problem evaluating the relative merits and de-merits of the traveller site's proximity to both local services and the river, crux of city's historic (read tourism) amenity. Precedent and protocol demanded that the twelve 'Known Families' be moved to a more appropriate location, following consultation with community leaders. There was uniform and minuted outrage at the discrediting use of the 'p-" word in the local (host) school's recent assembly on diversity. Put to a vote, it was not within the council's remit or budget to liaise with any possible recipient council. Their hands were tied.

Next day's cortege was a showstopper. Black Marias lined the route, clumsy acolytes to the dark, steaming horses. Flatbed trucks, suffocated with flowers, crawled ahead of a solitary, bow-topped, scarlet vardo which rolled in the rear like a defiant refugee from Hannah's imagination and Lucy's archived research. Some shops had their shutters down; most observers had their hands up, in front of their faces, capturing the cavalcade. Looking at the news pictures afterwards, seeing again the silence, Thomas thought they resembled evangelicals, hands raised to receive and pixellate the Holy Spirit. To Luce they were a collective representation of something organised and relevant.

Though Thomas hadn't really expected either girl to conjure an impromptu elegy, his address included a short extract from a poem by Donne instead of Herbert, just in case. As he spoke, he glanced up to the angels with their blank, Aunt Sally faces, forever flying, never falling, and heard his own voice curl disembodied through the public address system, unfolding itself to the enormous gathering, inside and out. The poem's words, private, ancient and familiar, rang around the airless, crowded church, escaped to the open and crept, faithful and expected, back to him. As they always did. Afterwards, Luce said he'd shown cultural sensitivity. She took his hand. The bell tolled its half dozen as the crowds dispersed and the mourners were sucked into The Moon & Sixpence like pebbles in the tide. Isaac asked if he could have big horses at Hannah's funeral.

Months later, after the Bailiffs had completed, a letter arrived at the vicarage for Doctor Father Thomas Avery, written on scented paper in large, looping script, not joined up. Although he was Gorgio, he was alright. They'd remember Queenie Bird forever. She had a good funeral. They liked the poem but if they ever came back, this would be better than what he'd said:

What's greater than God,
More evil than the Devil,
The poor have it
And the rich need it?

Nothing. No more. No signature, just the verse. Luce noted the postmark. Thomas let her keep it. Queenie Bird left nothing but her memory settled with them, forever.

Len's Whole Life

- Alice Kent -

Len looks at the time. 8.56 am. Something hurts. He smoothes down his tie. It is made of a brown, woolly carpet-like material. Nobody else has a tie made of this material. He checks around the office. He has never seen this material anywhere except as the material of his tie. Tuesday is the most common day for suicide. Eleven o'clock on a Tuesday. In June.

He checks his 'To Do' list: 'Fortify castle surrounding 6s'; 'Routine check of 3's army'; 'Consider additional security for 2s'. He presses a thumb against the spine of *The 7 Habits of Highly Effective People* aligning it perfectly with *Excel for Dummies*. He clicks on the Excel icon, opens a spreadsheet. Numbers that must be controlled. Only his numbers stir him. And when Carole from Accounts puts deodorant on when sitting at her desk, slipping her hand under her lilac silk blouse. Len smoothes down his tie. What is this fabric? When did he last buy a tie? To buy a tie, what an impossibility. His mother must have bought it for him.

He thinks of his mother's funeral. The roses in the chapel made of pink plastic with clear plastic rain drops stuck to the petals. Abide with Me. He thinks of the photo of him as a school boy that stood on his parents' television for over twenty years. People don't put photos on televisions anymore; they are too thin, the Tvs; people are fatter. 9.00 am. Eight hours, 7.5 hours, 0.5 for lunch.

Time is a modern construct.

He overhears the receptionist on the phone:

'Maybe, depends, what Sean says.'

'That's not fair, I came out the other week.'

'Ross, Sean means the world to me.'

Len leans forward and types with one finger s.e.a.n m.e.a.n.s t.h.e w.o.r.l.d t.o m.e. He sits back, looks at the words on the screen. Then he highlights the words and makes them 24pt and bold. Puts them in Batang font. Says 'Batang' out loud. Itches at the top of his left sock with his right foot. His socks dig too tightly and leave ridges, traces on his skin. No one knows this about Len, no one has seen the ridges his socks leave. He leans forward and types I w.a.n.n.a f.u.c.k s.e.a.n.s b.r.a.i.n.s o.u.t.

He scrambles to delete the text as Mr. Barnfield of Barnfield and Dyers appears at the side of his desk.

'Hello Len.'

Len clears his throat, smoothes his tie. 'Hello Mr. Barnfield of Barnfield and Dyers.'

'HA! You do make me laugh Len, got a minute?'

'Minutes, many I have.' Len's eyes sting.

On Mr. Barnfield's desk the folders containing Len's spreadsheets are stacked higher than the pile of poppadoms they had at the Rajdoot during the 2011 Christmas dinner. Martin from Marketing said there must be at least 15 poppadoms and then karate chopped them and Jayne from the Swindon office, who had missed out on promotion during the year she'd had to care for her husband who'd had throat cancer, said to be careful or he'd have them kicked out. 'Mr. Poppadom, Mr. fucking Poppadom,' Martin said in a comedy Indian accent.

'Len, it's somewhat awkward, but is everything ok? Are you under some kind of stress?' Mr. Barnfield leans forward and clasps his hands together to show Len he really cares.

KNOW THE SYMPTOMS OF STRESS warns the poster on the notice board in the communal kitchen. Know the symptoms of stress, then give blood, then sign the form to donate to Paul because he's jumping out of a parachute to raise money for a girl who needs to go to America for an operation, then rent Michelle's holiday house in Kent, then read the postcard from Pam who went to Tenerife. She retired last year, everyone misses Pam, and how she said Tener-re-fe. She had an amazing time and ate at her favourite taverna where Carlos greeted her and her husband as old friends and recommended the snapper.

'No, I'm not under any kind of stress Mr. Barnfield.'

Mr. Barnfield looks at Len in the same way Mr. Oakes did in primary school when he had to borrow the spare trousers they kept for accidents. They don't have spare trousers in offices. Len brings his own. Len looks at the photo of Mr. Barnfield and his wife on the desk. Mr. Barnfield is wearing a visor and a t-shirt that says, 'How's my driving? Call 800-100 GolfPro.' Mrs. Barnfield has large hoop earrings and her nose is scrunched up because she's smiling. Len wonders who took the photo. The person who takes the photo is always more interesting than the people in it. The voyeur. Who made Mrs. Barnfield smile like that? Mr. Barnfield sees Len looking at the photo.

'The Algarve last year, my brother has a place there.'

'Did he take the photo?'

'He? My brother? Yes, he probably did, or his wife.'

'Probably your brother.'

'Yes, probably Len. Now I need to talk about, this.' He taps the pile of folders.

'My work.' The words magnum opus swim in Len's head and the room sways slightly.

'Yes, Len, well listen, let's just look.'

Mr. Barnfield takes out the top spreadsheet from a stack of hundreds and puts it on the desk. Len has never fallen so quickly, fallen to where he is loved best of all. They depend on him for their very existence:

Those innocent 2s in Easter bonnets, all pale blues, yellows, Easter egg wrapping, made by a Bavarian Chocolatier who inherited the business from his father and his father before him, looking cute won't save them now, rock the babes; the 3s advance, their loyalty is legendary when they move they move as one, an army, a 3 crab line army advancing; 7s grab their 2s from the baskets and flee the city gates as cunning 5s who are good at heart, line up in defence; 4s never know which side to join, they can be all things to all people, perfectly divisible by 2 into 2, what more could anyone want? Yet, it is their burden. Only the 8s command real respect and Len holds them back; it has to be a good day for 8s to make an appearance. 8s know how to be, they don't have to pretend to be anything they are not. They end at the beginning and begin at the end. They start and finish with themselves.

To be an 8. Len can think of nothing finer. It brings tears to his eyes. When he sleeps he thinks of 8s. Follows the loops. The hopes and fears of all the years.

'Len, what is it all about?'

Len squints and looks at the spreadsheets carefully. 'It's pandemonium, Mr. Barnfield of Barnfield and Dyers.'

'Pandemonium?'

'The 8s aren't coming, the 7s won't get their 2s away in time and the 3s outnumber them, it's not good, it's not going to end well, there will be heavy losses I'm afraid.'

'Losses? Sales?'

Sales. The word hangs in the air between them. SALES enters in a tux, a fat belly, begins an aria, misses its cue, stands on stage guffaws, embarrassed it can't go back behind the curtain.

'Is it a forecast?'

Len thinks of the shipping forecast. The storm is moving slowly and losing its identity.

Mr. Barnfield leans back in his chair, lower belly hair protruding between his shirt buttons. Len blushes and wonders whether other people exist. Wonders what number Mr. Barnfield would be. God, what Len wouldn't give to be an 8, to start where he finishes, to finish where he starts. Mr. Barnfield would be a 2. He thinks of his enormous bulk, squashed in a Victorian pram, suckling on a dummy the size of his head, wearing a nappy, the swinging milk tits of a 7 bouncing off his chubby lips.

'Len, has something happened?'

Len thinks back, tries to remember. 'On Thursday the courier arrived with a parcel for Fran, she wasn't around to sign for it and so I signed for it for her.'

'And?'

'That's all.'

'Was there a problem? Was Fran ok? Has this upset you somehow?'

'No, it's just… I think that was the last thing that happened.'

'Len, that was nearly a week ago, I mean things happen all the time. What was wrong with the parcel? Did Fran receive the parcel ok?'

'It was a dressing gown from her mother.'

'So?'

'She'd kept the receipt so she could take it back if it wasn't the sort of thing Fran was after, she didn't know if she wanted something warm or something lacy. Fran thought Rick would probably have preferred something lacy. Carole from Accounts thought that was funny.'

'Why does any of this matter, Len?'

'It doesn't really.'

In the corner of the window behind Mr. Barnfield's head the leaves of the lime tree blow in a light wind and the sun glows at the edge of a cloud the shape of the Isle of Wight.

'Len the numbers don't add up.'

'No,' Len agrees.

'Why?'

'It's not finished yet.'

'What's not finished?'

'The War.'

'Len, you're acting quite peculiarly, I want you to take some leave. We value our employees here at Barnfield and Dyers and I want you to take all the time you need. We're a family firm, pride ourselves on that, and I won't have it said that we don't take mental health seriously. Most important thing we've got the old grey matter and it's nothing to be ashamed of.'

'Can I take the poppadoms home?'

Mr. Barnfield winces in incomprehension.

Len feels a sense of relief as he holds the files to his chest.

Outside the office Muspole Street is quiet. Water drips from the hanging baskets on the Frog and Whippet. The others will go there this evening because they do a weeknight meal deal of a bottle of wine and a wood-fired pizza. The pub has fake logs piled by the gas-effect wood burner. Len has never been to the pub but there are photos of them when sales were better than expected a couple of years back. The photos were put online so they could all remember the good time they had. Len remembers the day because it was when his fridge broke and he had to take all the cheese out and wrap it in the free Advertiser to keep it cool.

How many times has Len walked down Muspole Street to the bus stop? 4, 456 times. He wishes he had a record of all the things from the time of his birth. The number of times he has drunk a cup of tea, dialled for pizza, watched Countdown, held his mother's hand, masturbated, thought about going on a cruise, made a cheddar sandwich, lost the end of the cling film. Cried. If he had kept a record he could update it, put it on a spreadsheet.

Then everything would be in its place and no one would be left wondering. There would be no missing pieces to Len's biography. 18,800 slices of cheddar cheese for his sandwiches. Len's whole life.

Len wonders what the others in the office will be told. Maybe Mr. Dyer will get involved. Few people had met Mr. Dyer, but he joined conference calls sometimes. Graham from IT joked that there was no Mr. Dyer, that really Mr. Barnfield just ducked under the desk and pretended to speak through the conference-call speaker, but Susan who'd spent six months in the Swindon office said he existed alright, in a way that made her seem more interesting than anything she'd ever said before.

Len knows he should call the counsellor Mr. Barnfield has recommended, because he has to get things off his chest. He is showing signs of stress. DO NOT INGNORE THE SIGNS OF STRESS. The warning poster shows a cartoon cat with aching shoulders and her head in her hands. She has a migraine and shows signs of stress, which she plans to ignore.

Len runs his hand along the flint wall of the church that has stood here for over 800 years. He thinks of dunking witches, the plague, people wearing brown cloth, leather wrapped round their feet for shoes, eating soup with giant ladles. A brown, generic image of the past. How can they have actually existed? To start where you finish; to finish where you start.

In the distance the 9.59 bus pulls away. The next bus is at 10.59.

Just one hour to wait. Just sixty more minutes of life to be filled. 3,600 seconds. Not so much to count. Under the shelter of the bus stop, ignoring the school children sharing fags and the elderly unfolding plastic rain hats, Len counts out loud every second of the wait. And when the bus arrives at 10.59am on a Tuesday in June, Len steps out into the road. The bus stops just before him but expecting the impact he stumbles to the ground anyway. Blinking into the sun he looks up at the advert on the side of the bus. 'Text 'Sunny Daze Holidays' to 888 - The World is Your Oyster!' Len smiles and starts to get up.

The Girl I Left Behind

- Sarah Baxter -

I crouch over the loo, thighs tensed. The backless green gown skims my shins. A dribble of piss hits the water, not even an egg cupful. I brace my left elbow against my knee to keep the cannula straight.

A mirror, the length of the door, throws back my pathetic exertions. I'm bleached by the strip lighting. I've lost weight, my blue eyes are set in grey hollows. I bow forward, counterbalancing the drip stand and see stray hairs rebelling in my eyebrows. *Look at the state of you*, they say.

I bounce, shaking off the last drops; this is the lucky wee of a child before a long car journey. I chase the loo roll around its dispenser, performing a one-handed swirl to yank out the tissue. I wipe from front to back and realise I can't feel the paper against my skin. I rip another wad and wipe again. Nothing.

I run my hands down my shins, around my calves and over the tight skin of my ankle – nothing. I pinch the skin across my hips, the crease of my arse – nothing. I am alabaster from the waist down. I shuffle away from the toilet, my knickers stretched out between my ankles.

I add my body's topical apathy to the *fuck it* list of everything that's brought me to this bathroom, in a private hospital one street back from fashionable Darlinghurst.

I've been yo-yoing for years out of GPs' offices, first in London, then Sydney. Presenting with the vague symptoms of the dotcom generation – fatigue, pins and needles, blurred vision – I was consoled with a diagnosis of stress and ordered to take it easy. My flatmate, Nico, called an ambulance three days ago when I woke up with pain, like an axe in my skull, no colour vision and the legs of a fawn.

I knew I was fucked when the first doctor spent an hour testing my reflexes. He looked into my eyes with a pinprick torch. Flicked it left, then back, over and over.

"Grip my hands," he said. "Pull towards me."

I tried. And failed. He bleeped the on-call neurologist.

Dr Nielsen arrived three minutes later wearing his authority in the wool of his charcoal suit and sleek, white hair. He conferred with his underlings and asked me to walk up and down the cubicle. My trembling steps were the final clue.

"You have an abnormal gait," he said. "I believe you have demyelination in your thoracic vertebrae. You also have optic neuritis. I'm sending you for an MRI."

I felt a hot ball rise in my chest. I had graduated in medicinal chemistry and these years of study, which had previously only proved useful in Trivial Pursuit, meant I could translate his jargon. Demyelination was the answer. Dr Nielsen had incanted the word and bound me to it. I knew what myelin was, and what the lack of it meant.

"You're saying I have Multiple Sclerosis." It wasn't a question.

Dr Nielsen rocked back on his heels, "Yes. Do you need a minute?"

I didn't miss a beat, "No. I don't need a minute. I need you to tell me what to do and I need to get started."

His brow furrowed; I didn't fit the pattern of the customary weepy moment. I hadn't asked him for comfort or *why me?*

"OK. Come back to this hospital on Sunday. You'll be a patient for a week. We'll start you on steroids, then the MS medication and you'll feel better."

He turned to leave, but pivoted back as an afterthought.

"This is big news for anyone," Dr Nielsen whispered. "If the man outside this cubicle is the love of your life, then tell him. If not, leave him now." And, he was gone before I could form a smart-mouthed response.

I found Nico slumped in a grey plastic chair, his head tipped back against the wall.

"Hey, there," he said, running his fingers through his hair. "You ready?"

"Yup. Let's go home."

Nico offered the crook of his elbow and I linked arms, enjoying his solid bicep against my skin. We were easy flatmates, fitting surely into each other's lives. We'd been friends since we'd met at work, after I transferred from London for something better.

Nico didn't ask questions as we drove home over the Harbour Bridge. I knew he'd heard every word of my diagnosis and thought it wasn't worth unpicking.

There's a rap on the bathroom door.

"Are you alright?" a nurse asks. "Do you need a hand?"

"No. I'm coming," I reply, hastily hoicking up my knickers. The snap of elastic is unregistered against my skin. *I was right. I am bloody ill. I can't even feel my effing knicker elastic.*

I open the door and step onto the stage of this melodrama. Dr Nielsen, now acting as my official consultant, takes off his jacket. The nurse gestures for me to sit on the edge of the bed. It's not easy; the nurse and I perform an awkward dance with the drip stand. I bend forward, arms folded over a side table, exposing the target drawn in biro at the bottom of my spine. The nurse presses her hands flat against my shoulders, bracing me.

"Try not to move. Don't look at the needle," she soothes.

I'm not scared. My Nanna shared many wisdoms: how to rub fat into flour to make scones, how to get blood out of a hankie, and how to put a permanent crease in a man's trousers. She was from Norfolk farming stock, born into a lineage of women who got on with things. My family's motto could be, *Sometimes you have to get in the harness yourself, and pull.*

I am in the harness now, although I am tired in my bones – tired in the vitreous humour of my eyeballs and the *whump whump* under my ribs. A pain, from being punctured, blooms like vinegar.

"That's the anaesthetic. It'll numb in a moment. Keep still," Dr Nielsen reassures.

I am still. I am dust in a locked room.

There's a push and I imagine a tap is opened. Dr Nielsen finishes the procedure and the nurse lowers me onto the white sheets, one hand under my neck like a baptism.

"You must stay flat for eight hours, or you'll have the worst headache in the world," she promises.

I believe her and lay motionless, one arm pinned down by the saline drip.

"Can I see it?" I ask.

"What? Your spinal fluid?"

The nurse holds a vial of translucent liquid to the light. It's unremarkable. She zips the vial into a bag, and hands it to a porter. It'll give up its truth in the pathology lab – that I have MS and have crossed a threshold from which I can't return.

Nico stations himself in a high-backed chair. He leans over and we whisper like thieves. When the sodium glow of street lighting pushes its fingers through the blinds, he kisses my forehead goodbye. I fall asleep to the chatter of the portable TV.

I awake to the building's thrum. The room's other occupants, two elderly, bird-like women, are propped up against pillows in white dressing gowns. The blonde woman hasn't spoken since I arrived yesterday, but frequently passed my bed after dinner to top up a beaker with Chardonnay she'd stashed in the mini fridge. She is fair-skinned with a lattice of lines, earned from a lifetime under the sun, crisscrossing her neck.

The other woman is dark-haired and demanding. She calls out in a Zsa Zsa Gabor accent for more pillows or fresh water.

She eyed me with suspicion when I showed up with my suitcase.

"What are you here for?" she asked.

I explained slowly that I had Multiple Sclerosis, a disease of the nerves, and that I needed specialist treatment. The words didn't sound right in my mouth, they didn't belong.

"Nerves? What is wrong with your nerves? You shouldn't be here."

I realised *nerves* had been mistranslated as depression or addiction or feminine hysteria. I didn't bother to correct her.

I heave onto my elbows and ask an unfamiliar nurse to disconnect the drip. I need a shower. The nurses are colour-coded: agency workers wear light-blue cotton trouser suits or white, button-fronted dresses. The others wear stiff, navy dresses embellished with St. Vincent's insignia – a letter M, a flame and a crucifix enclosed in a shield. The significance is lost on my Protestant self. This nurse is definitely *agency*. She has a non-branded uniform and looks like she can't be arsed.

"You don't expect me to stay in bed all day, do you?" I ask rhetorically.

She unclips my silicone tether with a tut.

In the shower, I feel a bump at the base of my back - a Braille letter A for Anew, Abrupt, Alone. I dry my short brown hair with a stiff towel and put on my own uniform: khaki combat trousers, belted tightly with a plait of tan leather, battered grey Converses, and a red and white striped T-shirt which I tug over my inert hand with difficulty. I am necessarily bra-less.

The T-shirt stops short of a scar on my belly button from an old piercing. I unscrewed the diamanté-topped bar upon my arrival in Australia when I realised *everyone* had a pierced navel. The raw hole, like a catfish's mouth, sealed immediately.

After breakfast, the saline is replaced with a bag of steroids the colour of consommé to dampen the bushfire in my nerves. I am an international phone connection - my brain speaks, but my limbs only get the gist of the message through the time delay.

The bag's label reads *methylprednisolone*. It is the language of another country, the language I spoke when I was top in organic chemistry. It might as well be alchemy.

After an hour, I start to taste the steroid in my spit. I'm reminded of when an older boy at primary school dared me to lick the blade of a metal pencil sharpener.

I need decent coffee to mask the rise of chemicals. I unplug the drip from its socket and it kicks over to battery power, beeping in protest. I lean against the stand and wobble to the lifts, bound for the café on the ground floor.

As I pass the blonde patient, she calls out, "Darling, darling, are you going downstairs? You couldn't be a dear and get me a latte, could you? The coffee at breakfast tasted like rat shit. My purse is in the drawer."

She has a clear, singsong voice. Propped up on pillows, with a dressing covering an incision the length of her neck, she seems out of place with her gentle voice, plain language and savage wound.

There's a smattering of customers in the café. A young mother feeds her infant with a bright spoon and a pair of male doctors, ID badges tucked into their breast pockets, throw me sideways looks.

Connor, the barista, has sharp cheekbones and an on-trend haircut, shaved at the sides with a dark quiff. He's the type of guy that, even a week ago, I would have reeled in at a bar. It might have lasted for a few weeks, or maybe a night - either way it wouldn't have mattered. There were always more bars and other Connors.

This Connor meets my eyes with a neutral smile as he hands me an espresso. I throw the black liquid down my throat like an addict. The burn of coffee, and its aftertaste of ash and dirt, feels like shame under Connor's indifference; I have lost my sheen.

Back at the room Zsa Zsa's mattress has been stripped. I turn to Blondie, my eyes widening.

"Where is . . . ?" I ask hesitantly.

"Oh no, dear! Not that. She made a dreadful fuss. Said you brought a boy in here. She's in a private room."

Blondie continues, rolling her eyes, "Wasn't she a bore? Deaf as a post. We'll have more fun without her."

I set the latte down next to a stack of Blondie's style magazines.

"I can't stand this place. Sit here. We can be friends. I'm Margaret."

Margaret and I chat for hours, interrupted only by a bland lunch of quiche and new potatoes. Nico visits after work. He brings a Gladware box of cold penne arrabiata from his good Italian mother. I give him a shopping list: salted pretzels, a bag of Violet Crumble honeycomb and mandarins. My body craves essential tastes: salt, sweet and sour - I am a primordial creature being reborn. Margaret palms Nico twenty dollars for more wine and tells him to keep the change.

Later, Mike and Susan from my community choir arrive, bringing flowers and puzzle books. They wring their hands at my bedside, like a doom-laden chorus, and I'm relieved when they go.

Each morning, under Connor's continued indifference, I fetch coffee and I think *you're nothing to me* as I sashay forth with renewing strength.

Margaret and I cling together in the raft of our room. We pray we're spared from a third occupant to break up our love-in. Margaret has no family, no visitors. Her husband died in 1996 and she lives alone in Bondi.

"We didn't have kids. It just didn't happen. I have a twin; she lives in America. She had an abortion when she was twenty-three and the whole business put us off children," she explains.

"We didn't mind and neither did our husbands. They were too busy making money building Canberra. I hardly saw my Charlie. We had affairs, but as long as he never bumped into my chap in Sydney and I never met his girlfriend, it worked out."

Margaret pauses. "When Charlie died, he left me a very rich woman, but we never had time to enjoy it."

I touch her forearm. I'm glad my own family aren't here for reasons I don't voice.

"I've got two younger sisters. I rang Mum and asked her to tell them. I don't need them to do anything," I say.

Margaret shrugs. "If I've learned anything, it's that sometimes you're better off on your own, but you also need to know when to marshal your troops."

On the fourth day the steroid's art concludes and my strength flicks on like a light bulb, burning too brightly. I am resurrected like Lazarus of Bethany. I am cranked and ragingly hungry. My legs come back to me. All my feeling comes back to me. I am a bull stamping in the dust. I can't sleep. The night shift nurse brings a warm blanket and folds it around me like I'm an infant.

"Don't worry,' she whispers. "Everything's going to be OK."

At 4am I call Nico from the pay phone next to the nurses' station. I wait in the visitors' lounge.

Nico appears before dawn, his long curls pulled back in an elastic band. He's wearing a work shirt that needs ironing. We sit in the low arm chairs, hands clasped across the melamine table. I start to cry.

"What's the matter?" he asks.

What I don't say is, You fucking idiot, what d'you reckon? I couldn't walk. I couldn't feel when I pissed. That arsehole doctor stuck a needle so close to my spine I had to sign a disclaimer. And I'm a million miles from home. What else could be wrong?

This is unsaid because I need everyone and *anyone*. It's not Nico's fault that he's the anyone who showed up first.

"I don't know why I'm crying," I sob, cuffing the tears and snot away. "There's so much to do. And I want to do everything."

I gulp air.

"I want to . . . I don't know. I want to . . . ride a motorbike. I want to get a tattoo. I want to learn to fire a gun!"

I shout the third assertion while Nico strokes my inner wrist.

"You don't mean these things. It's the steroids talking. It'll be clearer next week," he pacifies.

I sniff in agreement to make him feel better. Nico leaves for work and I go back to the room.

On my last day in the hospital, a navy-blue nurse brings me the MS medication - a dozen pre-filled syringes in blister packs.

"That's it. Pinch the skin," she instructs.

"Like this, or a bit more?" I squeeze the top of my thigh, wishing I was fatter because the needle looks like something a vet would use.

"That's fine. Hold the point perpendicular and bounce it slightly. It'll help to ease it in."

I coax the metal through the stratum of my tissues and push the plunger. The suck of my flesh as the needle's withdrawn is unexpected.

The nurse continues her patter: relapses, the blood-brain barrier and how this medicine will protect me. But I don't care how it works; I don't care if it's a placebo. I'll do this three times a week and kiss the needle. The nurse leaves a pamphlet about support groups, which I throw away as soon as she's gone.

I swap addresses with Margaret and arrange lunch at the Diggers Club on Bondi Beach. She gets a discount because Charlie served in Korea. She says they make excellent counter meals and we can play the pokies.

Dr Nielsen comes to sign the discharge forms. He repeats the earlier reflex tests muttering "very good" each time. We sit on the bed and I smell his cologne, salty and ashen under his collar.

"Do you have any questions?"

"Not really," I shrug. "The nurse explained everything."

"Very good," he says again.

"There is one thing. It sounds stupid, but what am I supposed to do now?"

My question grows pregnant between us. Dr Nielsen smiles and tilts his head. The gesture makes him look younger.

"I'll see you in the outpatient clinic next week. Now, go home and live your life."

Suenos

- Susan Dean -

Dalila dreamt. She dreamt of many things but most often Dalila dreamt of sitting on the sea shore watching the surf curling over the sand. In her dream she had a notebook and pen and as she listened to the whispering wash of the advancing and retreating waves she was writing of her life as a poet, a poet like the Cuban hero, José Martí.

Dalila dreamt each day on her way to work. The journey from Santa Maria del Rosario in the Cotorro district into Habana Vieja, the city centre was a long one. The once yellow bus was crowded and uncomfortable and belched choking diesel fumes. Dalila's feet ached from her badly fitting shoes but for a while she could forget them and her surroundings, even the fumes that coated her tongue and stung her eyes.

She dreamt as she worked too, as she polished the windows on the seventh floor of the Hotel Habana Libre. If she had time to stop, Dalila could see the wide sweep of the Malecon through the windows, the long finger of land on the other side of the harbour with its fort and lighthouse and the open ocean beyond. But it wasn't the sea of her dreams. No, the sea of her dreams was far away, an impossible destination for a Cuban chambermaid.

After work Dalila would be too tired to dream. Some days she finished so late that a fat moon glanced down on the poorly lit city streets, illuminating puddles of water amidst the debris of the day, and from across the darkened bay the lighthouse sent her a compassionate wink. Clutching her scarf to her mouth, she would board the bus, rub one complaining foot against the other and perform a lurching samba to the whine of its engine all the way home. Home to prepare the evening meal, to cook and to clean, to listen to the grumbles of the old ones and the frequent arguments between her two small sons.

Dalila considered that without a doubt the best time of her life had been the all too brief years of childhood, a childhood that, on looking back, had been spent reading and writing. Her brothers had hated school, but not Dalila. The classrooms had been crowded and lessons taught by rote but there had been books: books to read and books to write in. Words on a blackboard or on a page had flowered and grown. The thrill of learning what they'd meant, the pleasure in a new notebook or a newly sharpened pencil, were things she remembered with poignant clarity. At home after school she'd searched out a quiet corner to read in. She'd devoured words, whole books of them. She'd been able to recite lines of prose in her head and had copied them down on to scraps of paper. When not reading or writing Dalila had dreamt of becoming an author.

But how could the daughter of a waiter aspire to be a novelist or a poet? When Dalila had completed her schooling she'd had to find work and had ended up washing dishes in a hotel kitchen. A fitting occupation for someone like her, so everybody had said. Then after a while, she'd met a young man, Yunier, a waiter like her father. She'd imagined that the passionate feeling she'd suddenly felt for him had been true love, and so they'd married.

Marriage was not as Dalila had imagined. Where was the romance she'd read about in so many books? Where were the tender words? Where was the life of contented harmony she'd expected? Her own parents had been happy enough. But she and Yunior?

She'd fallen pregnant almost immediately and could remember looking at herself in the cracked mirror propped against the wall on the battered set of drawers in their one rented room, wondering if Yunier was right. Was she really so unattractive, so unsatisfactory as a wife? The face that gazed back at her had been recognisably hers: wide cheekbones, large dark eyes, broad nose, full lips, but was her skin too dark? Her long black hair too severely tied back? She'd become quieter – true - but she'd quickly learnt that to contradict Yunier prolonged the petty arguments then the silences.

Their room in the city centre hadn't been big enough for three so, following the birth of their son, Dalila had given up her job and they'd moved in with Yunier's parents and extended family, far out in the suburbs. Housing was scarce everywhere in the city and she and Yunier had had no savings, no choice. The large three storey house in Santa Maria del Rosario had once been magnificent, but now was uninviting and crowded.

'It is beyond repair, damp and crumbling,' Dalilia had told her mother, 'and it's full of people.'

Her mother hadn't been sympathetic. 'Think yourself lucky. You can share the cooking and child care and there will be plenty of people around at festival times.'

Yunier's family had taken some getting used to though. There had been more arguments than laughter, more noise, and no place to retreat to with a book or to dream. 'But what do you want with a book?' her father-in-law had asked. Dalila had felt a pang of despair but said nothing.

Another son had been born and for a while Dalila felt happy. She'd sung to her babies, told them stories, tales of magic, and whispered lines of poetry to them while they'd slept. She'd held their curled fists in her hand and for a time the desire to hold a pen and to write went away. But the arguments with Yunier hadn't stopped, if anything had got worse, and the subsequent silences more prolonged. Eventually he left her for another woman; a woman he'd described as 'Una mujer de verdad', a woman of some substance with a home of her own in Vedado.

For a while, except for the absence of her husband in her bed, life had continued much the same. Then Dalila's brother-in-law secured a new job in a tourist hotel in Santa Clara. He found rooms to rent there and called for his wife and their children to join him. Dalila suddenly found herself responsible for two small sons, two aging parents-in-law and even older grandparents.

What Dalila might have wanted counted for nothing. She had

learnt in school that Cuban women had equal rights with men in all areas of life: economic, political, cultural, social and in the family. It said so in article forty-four of the Cuban constitution. But constitutional rights made little difference in real life. She could only concur silently with her father-in-law who said, 'My son was right, you are useless, always daydreaming. No good as a wife. No sirves para nada.' Dreams of writing had to be put aside and she would have to find a full time job.

Dalila didn't like the featureless concrete façade of the hotel Habana Libre but did like the idea that it had once been the Habana Hilton and for a while Castro's headquarters. She had learnt at school about the revolution and his three month stay in suite 2324, several floors above the seventh to which she was assigned to make beds and wash windows, clean baths and change towels. Her life was exhausting. When not working there was the house in Santa Maria del Rosario to look after and the family to care for. On the bus into work, Dalila sometimes dreamt of escape.

The guests were mostly tourists, for few in Cuba had the money to stay in a hotel. Dalila noticed them with interest and weaved stories around them. Some were very ordinary, others not. Many were fat and obviously wealthy. Some left a tip, some did not. Some kept their rooms tidy, others did not. They arrived and then they departed, leaving without a trace for places Dalila couldn't visualise. Far-away places: Spain, England, Canada, Venezuela. Dalila's English was less than basic and the tourists, unless from Spain or Venezuela, could speak little Spanish, so most stayed and then departed with only a single word spoken, 'gracias'. Why would anyone want to talk to a simple chambermaid?

One day, a tourist, a woman on her own, arrived to stay. Two weeks in room 707, a room with a view of the city and the Malecon. Dalila, putting towels in the bathroom when she arrived, was startled when the woman wheeled her suitcase into the room and called out a greeting, 'Hola.' The woman had a kind, open face and a friendly smile. Dalila tried to guess her age but found it difficult. She had white hair but didn't seem in the least bit old.

In the days that followed the woman would stop in the corridor if she saw Dalila trundling her cart of towels and cleaning equipment from room to room. 'Hola,' she would say, then make some remark in English that Dalila couldn't understand.

"Hola,' Dalila would reply, and they would stand and simply smile at each other, as though each had, by mutual consent, given up the unequal task of trying to make further conversation.

At the end of the first week the woman gave Dalila twenty pesos for ironing a blouse and four tee shirts. It was a large amount of money to give for something that Dalila would willingly have done freely. It was enough for Dalila that the woman had noticed her, had smiled and said many times 'hola' and 'gracias'.

More importantly, it seemed that the woman was a writer. The evidence was there for Dalila to see when she cleaned her room, for on the bedside table lay a fine-looking fat notebook and an elegant gold pen. Dalila would pick them up, would feel the weight of the pen and breathe in the animal fragrance of the leather-bound book. How different they were from her own scraps of paper and chewed stub of pencil. Each day the woman wrote. Sometimes a page, often more. Pages of sloping writing, as elegant as the gold pen that supplied the ink. The words looked beautiful and important even if Dalila couldn't understand them.

At the start of the second week Dalila decided to give the woman a poem. She didn't want her to leave without knowing that she, Dalila, the chambermaid, was a writer too. Her friend Carmen, who worked at the reception desk of the hotel, was persuaded to provide a single sheet of crisp, white paper and at her lunch break Dalila took the paper and her newly sharpened pencil to a quiet corner of the hotel lobby. It was a poem that had came to her a year or so before, a poem she had recited in her head so often that she knew it by heart. She wrote each line with great care. The poem told of her dream life as a poet, of sitting on the sea shore, looking at the sea, words tumbling out of her head onto pristine paper. It told of her real life: the hotel, children, responsibilities. It told how by some means the two had got muddled up. How her real life should be that of the poet, the life she lived each day - a dream. How somehow the dream she had stumbled into had become a nightmare, a nightmare she was unable to escape from. How all she longed for was to return to her real life on the sea shore.

The woman found the poem and asked, 'Español al Ingles por favor?' Her Spanish was very poor but Dalila understood enough and cursed herself for her foolishness. She should have realised. Of course she would try to find someone to translate the words. Dalila and the woman looked at each other in frustration. There were so many things each wanted to say and to ask: Where do you live? What is your life like? What do you write about? Why do you write?' They needed words to communicate but where were the words? The words that both so obviously loved were an insurmountable barrier between them.

With the help of some coaching from Carmen, Dalila finally managed to ask in broken English, 'What do you write each day. Que es lo que escribe cada dia?'

'Things I see, things I hear, what I notice about Cuba and its people.' The woman replied in English, talking slowly with hand gestures so that Dalila could understand. 'And you? What do you write?'

'It is hard,' was all Dalila could say in English. 'I work. I have to get money.' What she wanted to say was that it was hard when all she wanted to do was write down the thoughts that filled her mind. How life was hard to bear when all she wanted was to leave the real world she inhabited for the dream world of the poet and the writer.

At the end of her stay the woman left another twenty pesos. She took the piece of paper on which Dalila had written her address, folded it up with the poem and put both carefully in her bag. She promised that she would send pens and notebooks. She smiled at Dalila, hugged her. For a moment Dalila could imagine that anything, just anything, was possible.

Dalila could have spent the twenty pesos on a notebook and pen. Both were hard to come by in Cuba but could be bought. There were many other needs though. Shoes for her sons, light bulbs, extra meat. All the things her meagre wages did not cover and that did not come in the monthly rations from the government.

Dalila did not doubt that the woman had kept her word and that the pens and books had been sent but they did not arrive. Dalila was not surprised. It was the way of things in Cuba. Dreams were meant to be just that: *sueños*, dreams.

Quick Brown Fox

- Kim Sherwood -

A thin is the width of a perfect 's' or as near as dammit. Two thins will be bigger than one thick. You want the spacing so when you tip the letters back, forty-five degrees, the type stays put. Keep a thumb as a sure guard. Otherwise your letters will fall all over the floor, and that's what we call letterpress pie.

Said all that in the beginning, didn't I? The girl trying it out laughed at the pie. Her hands were cold to the touch when I arranged 'em on the composing stick – in the same way, she asked, as you hold the frog of a cello bow. And then swapped a glance with her friend, as if to say, shouldn't have asked him that about the cello, he won't know. They're on 'j' now but neither of 'em can find it. Lower case is on the left as we have it here, remember. You're looking for a small box, up near your bracket and your Latin ligature, 'cause you don't need a 'j' too often. That's it. Not like your QWERTY, this. 'Q' at the bottom with your periods and quads. Right up there on a typewriter, top row. Both of 'em smile and I add, *keyboards* too. Only got one computer in this place and it's in our library, behind lithography. Everything in here is printed the proper way, pre-computerisation. Pamphlet over there on the wall, the forgotten art of the punchcutter, did that with the 'press. The Christmas cards, that's 'press and risograph. No we'd not sell 'em, we take some orders, carols, funerals, community stuff. Mostly just do it for ourselves, though. All the boys in here worked the trades before computers, digital this and digital that.

'And Marie, who's book-binding,' I add, giving them a conscientious smile. I get a we-know-you're-being-conscientious-smile back.

'Do you ever teach the public?' the friend watching asks. 'Let people come in and learn properly, print their own things?'

'We get some art students – you doing art at the uni?'

'No, literature.' They're MA students. 'What kind of literature?' Both look awkward.

'I'm reading Early Modern Poetry,' the friend says.

'And I'm actually, I'm a writer, studying creative writing, I mean,' says the girl at the stick, looking even more embarrassed. 'I guess I write the poetry and you study it.' They share a sudden laugh, all enthusiasm: 'We were so excited to hear about this place.' The laugh drops off.

Well then. Know why it's called upper case and lower case? When they switched from trying to reproduce monk's handwriting to Roman letters (but Arabic numbers, Roman letters and Arabic numbers), they put the capitals in the case up top, and the rest down here in the lower –

'Oh, upper case and lower case,' says the poet. 'I never knew that. How amazing.'

She's quick to find the 'u', bottom left, don't need no help from me, so I tell them, say, I went into printing as an apprentice before being called up. We're supposed to chat to 'em, make 'em feel welcome – even then, when Mike's on the door he warns folk you can't shut us up. Last year of the war, I tell 'em. Royal Signals. S'pose they thought my work in the 'press was extra training, much as the army thinks – but it weren't training for Bren guns and hallucinating from anti-tetanus. That's all Signalling was those first six weeks in Glasgow, then Yorkshire moors, then a few months 'round Normandy. Never been back, not to any of 'em. I'm a local boy.

The poet gives me a look. Should've just said France like always, don't know why I didn't. 'Normandy' makes people feel obliged, like they've got to ask questions, and she's looking at the red poppy in my buttonhole now. Never been back to any of 'em. One mouthful of salted Scottish porridge was enough to settle that. Her pinched expression relaxes. Ended up an OWL B2. Know what that is? Operator Wireless and Line. Taught us Morse. Same rhythm as the 'press, almost. Ways to remember the letters. 'Q' – tap it out – dah dah dit dah. Here comes the bride. Frowns from both of 'em, but that's right, here comes the – oh, the corporal what taught us would say: treat your brides as queens, lads, as queens. Here comes the bride, here comes the queen, 'Q'. Dah dah dit dah. Don't know if I recall any others, except 'L': *didit 'urt cher? Like 'ell it did.* 'Ell for 'L', that's right. Dit dit dah dit.

They're on 'm' now.

Came back to the 'press, of course. Only stopped when it closed down in '75. Kind of like we were courting each other, in the end: when I retired from the telephone 'change the 'press opened up again as a museum, so I started to volunteer. '93, that was.

Can't find the 'm'.

When I was apprenticed you had to know the letters by the feel of your thumb with no looking – their eyes on my thumb now as I stroke the 'm', but it's too inky, rub it against my shirt and feel again; *is* that an 'm'? Could be an 'n'. Tourists always distributing wrong. Wide, impressed eyes dimming with sympathy now. Feel the nick on top, where's the nick, now stroke down the type into the dip of lead, 'm' or 'n', double arch or single, double or– I've lost it, my fingers have lost it. It's on the floor. Girl gets there quick and offers it out to me and I'm groping in her hand for the type. Never dropped nothing in front of public before. Used to be able to do this with point four… Point three, even. Point three.

'p', 's', 'o'…

'How do you remember where they are in the case?' the poet asks, finding the 'v' and 'f', and it's pity in her question – covering up pity. I tell 'em just like you and your touch screens and your phones. Get to do it automatic. My wife was a secretary; she can do those QWERTY keyboards without once looking down. Learnt with a bag over her head – that's right, a sack, they put music on and a sack over your head and it was words per minute, words per minute. Just her breathing in the dark. The sack would be damp by the end from her sweat.

The early modern girl makes a polite, really, *wow*, interrupted by the poet: 'It's standing up!' Yes, it is, forty-five degrees, every letter in its place. Done.

'Just did the spacing like I showed you in the start, I s'pose, copying.' It's not the words of a guide or a teacher, words I'd use for my kids. It's little, and I'm little in that moment I know.

'The quick brown fox jumps over the lazy dog,' reads the poet. 'Why do fonts always say that when you download them?'

'It's every letter of the alphabet.'

Uni students so we refuse their donations, don't take money from you lot 'cause we know you ain't got none. Just sign the guest book; we don't let anyone go without signing the guest book. You know what word is used most often in there? 'Fascinating.' Most people say it's 'fascinating'. It really is, they agree, and pause with their pens, finding another word. The poet looks back at the 'press – not minding what she's writing in ballpoint (no ink nib, I heard Bill ask her over at pen-ruling), a blue ballpoint that now writes unwatched, *so good the museum exists because it's a piece of living history* – she looks back at the 'press and says, 'I never worked that out before, the brown fox. That's brilliant.' She's a Creative Writing Masters student and it's brilliant, she says, that quick brown fox and that lazy dog.

'Know what Benjamin Franklin said? Give me twenty-six soldiers of lead and I can conquer the world.'

She says that's brilliant too and I don't tell her it probably wasn't Franklin, could have been Marx, could have been some Frenchman, could have been the bloody fox.

My Sister's Haircut

- Dani Redd -

When I was twelve years old I heard my sister and her friends talking about fingering. I found out what it meant but the word didn't sound very sexy to me. It reminded me of the movement a worm or a caterpillar would make as it inched along a hard surface. And when I tried this movement in my bedroom the first feeling was not desire, but shock. Shock that there were so many bumps in there and that the route my finger had to follow curved round as if it was beckoning to someone. I'd expected a smooth, straight passage and worried that I was unnatural and if a boy ever stuck it in there the angle might break it.

I'd heard them talking about hard-ons too. Whenever I saw couples holding hands or kissing I always wondered if the boy had one, an idea that was disconcerting and fascinating in equal measure. How would I behave if I ever got to kiss a boy and felt that pressing against my leg? Was I meant to rub myself against it? Or was I supposed to ignore it, pretend it wasn't there?

I tried to learn by watching my sister. She was five years older than me and there was a steady stream of boys interested in her. I didn't always see them. They were the shadows wrapped round her on the pavement outside late at night or the gruff nervous voices asking for her on the phone. Sometimes they were no more than the same name repeated over and over when she spoke to friends, spoken with the type of awe reserved for discussing a mythical creature. Then abruptly that name would disappear and another one would materialize.

Daniel began in the same way as the others, as little more than a whisper. But then, unlike the others, he became a man standing on our doorstep and a hulking presence at the dinner table. I remember how wild and out of place he looked with all those earrings and hair as dark and tangled as seaweed.

I caught them kissing on the sofa once, his face mashed against hers. One hand was wrapped in her hair and the other was burrowing underneath her top, scrabbling for a flesh- hold. I stood in the doorway and watched them until they noticed me and told me to go away. After that I daydreamed of having a boyfriend like Daniel. But the dream-man's feet didn't smell like Daniel's when he took his boots off in the hallway and his nose was different; more chiselled, less like a blob of dough. In fact maybe he looked more like Johnny Depp. But still, he kissed me exactly the same way I'd seen Daniel kiss my sister.

It was obvious how Hattie felt. Her eyes were entirely naked when she looked at him; two baby mice that squeaked with need. Whenever our parents went out she'd be straight on the phone to him and he'd arrive on the doorstep, red-faced and doubled-over, panting. Their footsteps would thunder up the stairs. The bedroom door would slam. Our bedrooms were next to each other and through the adjoining wall I could hear sucking sounds and the shrill giggles she produced only for him. Then I'd hear soft groans and the bedsprings would begin to creak, slowly at first, and then faster and faster until the gasped-out ending. I wondered how long I'd have to wait until someone touched me the way he touched her.

Walking home just before sunset one day, I saw Daniel on the other side of the road. The light was a strange grey-gold and it made his skin look sallow. He was staring straight ahead, lips pressed tight together, jaw clenched. He looked too big to fit in the houses even though they were all two storeys high. And he looked too unkempt for the miniature squares of lawn that lay side-by-side all down the street, separated by neatly clipped privet hedges. I waved but he didn't see. At any rate he didn't wave back or acknowledge me in any way. His elongated purple shadow tugged at his heels as he strode past me. I turned and watched as he rounded the corner and disappeared from sight.

In the house Hattie was crying on the sofa.

'What's wrong? Is it Daniel?'

'Yes,' she choked out, which caused another fit of sobbing.

'He broke up with you?'

'No. He wants me to get a haircut.'

Hattie cried easily but I wasn't sure why she was upset now.

'That's alright, isn't it?'

'No, dummy. He wants to cut it all off. He says whenever he has a girlfriend he likes them to shave their heads.'

'Why?'

'He thinks it makes them look fit. Like Tank Girl.'

'Who's Tank Girl?'

'Never mind,' she sighed, turning her face away from me.

'So, what are you going to do?'

'I don't want him to stop fancying me. I think I'll have to.'

'Are you sure?'

'No.'

'Mum will go ballistic.'

'Who cares?'

'But,' I said, sensing her growing annoyance, 'at least hair grows back.'

'Yeah,' she said, 'and I can always wear a hat.'

The next day I was in my bedroom reading when I heard the sound of footsteps on the landing. They stopped outside my door.

'Ellie, can you do me a favour?' Hattie called.

I opened the door.

'What?'

'Daniel wants you to shave my head.'

'Why can't he do it?'

'He wants to take photos.'

'I can take the photos. I might shave your head wrong. I've never done it before.'

'Dan? Can Ellie take the photos instead?'

He emerged from the bathroom holding an electric razor in one hand and a pair of scissors in the other. He looked dangerous. My ideal boyfriend would never make me shave my head, I thought.

'Come on Ellie, you can do it. It'll be fun,' he pleaded.

'It won't. I don't see why I can't take the photos and you shave her.'

'No,' he snapped at me, 'I need to watch.'

'Why?'

He didn't answer. I looked imploringly at Hattie, but she avoided my eyes.

'Please, Ellie,' he said.

'Please,' she echoed faintly.

Being able to say 'no' was something I hadn't learnt yet.

In the bathroom Hattie sat on the toilet and I stood to one side of her. Daniel perched on the side of the bath and watched us, camera in hand. With one hand I clutched strands of long brown hair. The scissors I was holding in the other flashed in the light as they made the first cut.

'Closer to the scalp,' Daniel said, 'otherwise the hair will get stuck in the razor when you shave it.'

The dark strands fluttered downwards, soft as ash. Some landed on the floor; some snagged on Hattie's shoulders. Her eyes were wet as she saw the hair fall away. Daniel took photo after photo, never once leaving his spot on the side of the bath. I felt shy; I'd never been observed so intently before.

I cut and cut and eventually the long strands were gone and we were surrounded by a nest of fallen hair and Hattie's face was lightly coated in it too, a network of strands like cracks. She looked pale and scared.

'Now for the razor,' he said.

Hattie jumped as he turned it on and it buzzed loudly in his hand.

'Don't worry,' he told her huskily, 'it doesn't hurt.'

He kissed her forehead. She began to cry.

'Maybe I should stop?' I suggested.

'It's too late for that now. You might as well finish it,' Hattie said.

She closed her eyes as Daniel showed me how to use the razor. I made one tentative movement across Hattie's scalp, creating an oblong patch of prickles.

'Was that ok? Did I hurt you?'

'No.'

I continued. The razor vibrated against my hand. It was an uncomfortable feeling but I didn't want to let go. I felt powerful standing above her, my actions revealing Hattie's scalp in all its pale uneven boniness. In that moment she wasn't my older sister anymore, my pretty older sister with the curls that shone like wet conkers in sunlight. She was a defenceless shuddering creature. The top of her head was startling to look at; a stone rounded by the sea, with flecks of dandruff beginning to dislodge from its surface. The stone tilted sideways.

'Keep your head straight,' I told her.

Ordering her around felt like winning a race; something that rarely happened.

I glanced over at Daniel and saw him swallow rapidly. His lips were parted and slightly moist. Our eyes met. My stomach clenched.

I finished and Hattie stood up. Her eyes were still red-rimmed. She seemed vulnerable and ageless. She looked in the mirror at herself and Daniel started taking photos of the back of her head and the nape of her neck. I watched them both, unnoticed and still grasping the razor. Hattie wasn't paying attention to either of us. She was mesmerised by herself, tracing the contours of her skull with her fingertips.

'My head feels so much lighter. I could get used to it.'

'Good,' he said, 'because I like it.'

He stood behind her, pressed himself tight into her back and started stroking her head with his hands.

'Ellie, you can go now,' she told me, still looking in the mirror.

Daniel began to kiss her neck. I was no longer useful.

'Shall I get a dustpan and brush for the hair?'

'No,' he said quickly, 'I'll do it.'

They slammed the door behind me. I ran to my bedroom and threw myself face-down on the bed. It wasn't fair. I grabbed handfuls of the duvet and began to move my hips in circles, grinding my crotch against the mattress in anger and frustration.

Later when I went to the bathroom the hair was gone. It wasn't in the bathroom bin, or the one in the kitchen. When I asked Hattie where it was she shrugged and changed the subject.

Hattie told me that being bald felt amazing. She loved feeling the sun and the rain against her scalp. She told me that if you leant very lightly against something the little bristles of hair could sense it and it felt like being stroked all over the top of your head. The only time this increased sensitivity annoyed her was when it was cold. Then she had to wear a hat. Needless to say, our parents were angry when they saw her new haircut although I heard them laughing about it later after they'd gotten over the shock.

I heard Hattie tell one of her friends that she liked the way her new haircut shocked people. On our street the rows of pasty middle-aged men who all washed their cars at the same time on Sunday stopped to stare as she passed. The old people, picking their way across the soap-streaked pavements, sucked in their breath when they saw her. When I walked past they didn't even turn their heads.

So she bought the clothes to match. Laddered tights, clunky boots, ex-army jackets. But then her hair started to grow back. She told Daniel she wouldn't shave it again because she was going to university in September and she didn't want anyone to get the wrong idea about her. He couldn't persuade her to change her mind. And then he was gone, so suddenly that it almost felt like magic; the only traces he'd been there the salty tear-trails that marked Hattie's cheeks for days after.

I was relieved. It was a lot simpler when it was just me, her and our parents. Despite the tears she was nicer without him; less moody and distracted. And perhaps I was nicer without him too. It was a relief not to have him staring at her across the dinner table, or to hear those sounds through the wall. I felt, for some reason, as if I could breathe more easily. All this surprised me because I'd thought, originally, that I would miss him.

A month or so after Daniel left our parents took us out to an expensive restaurant to celebrate Hattie's exam results. Her hair had grown into a sleek pixie cut and she was wearing jeans and a flowery patterned shirt. Our dad kept on remarking how nice she looked. Hattie smiled and said, 'thank you, thank you,' and drank her glass of wine a little too fast. She asked for another. And then another.

Later that night she came into my room.

'I want my hair back,' she whispered, sitting on my bed.

'What do you mean? It's growing back.'

'No, dummy. The hair that was cut off. Daniel has it.'

'Why?'

'I think he likes to… well, never mind. You're too young to understand.'

'How do you know?'

My head filled with images of what Daniel could be doing with the hair. I had recently discovered how it felt to put soft, silky things against that spot between your legs, and I was sure he knew about that too.

'I just do. But anyway I don't want him to have it. It feels weird.'

Suddenly I felt wide awake. 'Let's go and get it.'

'What, now?'

'Why not? We can knock on his window and make him give it to us.'

'It's late.'

'So? He'll be awake.'

It was summer and it hadn't been dark for very long. The sky was a bruised purple colour. It hung above the houses and they looked unfamiliar even though I saw them every day. I knew every curve in my street intimately, but tonight it felt as if we were passing into dangerous, unexplored territory. I ran my hand along a wall, feeling the sun's heat still trapped inside each brick. My feet tapped out erratic impatient rhythms against the tarmac.

My sister stumbled. She cursed and said this was stupid, she wanted to go back home. I told her we couldn't. I was going through a contrary phase. My breasts had started to grow and the bumps itched all the time and I imagined scratching them open and wings unfolding from them, or roses. I wanted excitement and it seemed that nothing ever happened to me, so I was not going to let this opportunity pass me by.

Daniel lived in a bungalow with his elderly aunt and his bedroom overlooked the garden. But Hattie stopped outside the garden gate and clutched it for support.

'I want to go home,' she repeated.

'But we're here now. Come on,' I whispered.

'He's going to think I want him back, coming this late.'

'Not with me here.'

I pushed open the gate and she reached out and gripped my arm. I led her forwards and then felt my stomach clench with nerves. I was filled with sudden confusion and half-wished I hadn't talked Hattie into this. But I was too proud to tell her that, or too stupid, or both. And besides, my curiosity had become insatiable.

The curtains were open and a light was on inside his room. Our shadows were spidery on the illuminated square of lawn. She stepped in front of me. Her shadow inched its way towards the window. She gasped. The sound made me rush to join her.

Daniel was fast asleep on his bed. He was curled up on his side, legs at right angles from his body. His face looked softer; younger than usual. I stared at him.

'Why did you gasp?'

'Look at what he's holding.'

I looked. Her hair was entwined round his fingers and he was clutching it tightly. It didn't look like Hattie's hair anymore. It looked like a small animal, curled and silken against his cheek. There was nothing dangerous or scary about it at all. I felt my stomach plummet with disappointment. He just wanted something to hold onto to remind him of Hattie. It was as pitiful as catching him sleeping with a teddy bear.

'Should we wake him and get it back then?' I asked my sister, hoping at least to enliven the evening with a conflict.

'I'll go back tomorrow. If we wake him he'll shout blue murder. Anyway, how're we going to get in? The window's closed.'

She walked away and as usual I followed. Back past the squat little bungalows that studded his street, and all the cars parked parallel on the driveways. We turned into the street where the terraces began. They looked like they'd been cut from the same piece of paper, joined together just the same as they always had.

'In a weird way that was sort of cute, don't you think?' Hattie asked.

'No. It was pathetic,' I replied, with a vehemence that startled us both.

As I said this something curled up in my chest and ossified there. This thing re-appeared from time to time over the following years. It was there the first time I was fingered, when after all that yearning I knew I could have done it better myself. It was there after my first time when I stood in the bathroom and looked at the used condom in the bin, curled up limply on a bed of tissue, and thought 'that's all?'

But the first experience of it was the most intense, that night we left Daniel's. That night when everything drained away and came back harder; less like a liquid, more like stone. That night when we walked the rest of the way home in silence, our feet thudding hollowly against the tarmac. When the streetlight on the corner winked at me; once, twice, and then went out.

For The Records

- Lois Williams -

[A-side]

The girl who plays Liesl Von Trapp is singing about numbers –
sixteen, seventeen – and my throat is on fire. Seventeen seems a
long way off. I'm seven, going on eight. My mother is in the kitchen
making a cake and I can hear her fork chasing the eggs around the
bowl. She's singing too. The record player is in the kitchen with
her, and a stack of LPs from when she and my father used to go
out. Liesl sings, and my mother sings backup. Something about
someone who's old and wise. Everyone on our road is old. A girl
at school has told me that my mother is old. Too old for another
baby. It is 1975 but it might be 1957 in our house, where we live,
on a windy headland near the Wash.

I have memorized a good portion of Rodgers & Hammerstein's
lyrics from being off school sick so much: *Oklahoma!*, *South Pacific*,
the songs of far flung places. These are the tunes I hear my parents
singing – these and 'Blue Skies', and my father's stuck-in-his-head
song by Charles Aznavour. I find them dancing around the house to
it on Sundays before he leaves us again. Sometimes after this song
he calls her Trish or she calls him Peter. *Go and see what Trish is up to*,
he'll say to me. *Your mother. Go and see if she needs a hand.* This is how
it goes in our house. We are always looking to see if anyone needs a
hand, as if two hands are not enough.

Doctor Ah has come to peer into my mouth. Deep breath, he says. Say aaah. He clicks open the latches of his doctor's case, a moment of transport, like the click of Dorothy's heels. My head hurts with fever but I can't resist studying the contents: wooden spatulas, a hammer for making knees jump, and a stethoscope, which he'll drop back in – an eel into a bucket. Tonsillitis, he concludes.

This time he tells my mother that I'll need to have them out. He looks Von Trapp serious, but I've heard the record enough times to know that the baron has many beautiful songs inside his chest. He is tall and dark-haired, and has no idea that I've cast him in the role of leading man while my father works away from us the other side of London. He picks up his case, nods to my mother. There's a moment when I think he might kiss me goodbye, as my father would, or sing farewell, but he merely leaves.

The adult world is full of mysteries. When I'm sick these mysteries become more pronounced and, if I listen closely, more a language I might one day learn to speak. Marguerite from across the road comes over to see how I am faring. She knocks on the kitchen door and hands a tray of junket to my mother. For her throat, she says. I dread Marguerite's junket. I dread her thoughtfulness at making it and the grey gelatinous curdled milk it consists of, and my mother's inability to refuse it. Thank you, my mother says. How kind of you.

We have an agreement that I don't have to eat the junket. I ate it once and told her it felt like snot in my mouth, which surprised her. She forgets I have an older brother. I don't see why she doesn't say to Marguerite please not to make any more, instead of accepting it, then eating it herself and sliding the last of it down the sink.

To cheer me up, she tells me that I'm like her sister Peggy. I have all the ailments nobody ever dies of. When they are girls, Peggy is sent to have her tonsils out, and my mother, whose tonsils are perfectly well-behaved, is sent along for company to have hers out too. She tells the story to me in the present tense, and somehow this is the right medicine – a kind of hypnotic, making me a sister too. She and Peggy are sent to sit in a dark room in only their vests and knickers, with other children who keep getting colds. A nurse switches on a sunray lamp and the children circle around it like small animals coming out of a forest. Peggy loves it. She reclines in the warm light. The lamp's glow turns her skin golden brown. Twice a week for half an hour she is Coco Chanel. My mother hates it. The windowless room and goggles when she'd rather be outside. The way her skin itches afterwards. The itch that makes her think of cockroaches.

My mother is saved from this misery by the midwife, who checks on my grandmother after a recent delivery and finds the baby well and Patty red-faced and fiery. Patty has the ginger skin, she tells my grandmother. No more sunray treatment for Patty.

And it ends, just like that.

Not dying has its compensations. Dr Ah writes me a week off school, *confined* he calls it, so that I might get back my resistance (another of his words). Away from school the time feels secret, filled with my mother and the record player. The house has a rhythm of chores and food, and behind this floats the music, which makes everything a play. On Tuesdays the bread man brings us a large white and a Hovis. On one of these visits I notice that the tip of his finger is missing. Was it in the bread? A shock of almost-pain flares in my own hand at what might have happened. And then the music distracts us. A woman is singing about washing her hair. A man is in her hair and she is going to wash him out. I look into the bread man's face; he knows the tune. His face has brightened up. He could be one of my grandfathers after a win on the horses. He doesn't seem to notice his lost finger, so I try to stop noticing it too. I decide that he must have lost it in the war. The war is the lockbox of missing things.

[B-side]

I think of those days now as confinements in the old-fashioned sense of that word: days just prior to a birth when the woman is away from the world, in a world of her own. They share similar qualities of remove and concentration. Outside, the public day went along: my father on a building site somewhere far from the sea, my brother and my friends walking to school, taking the short cuts that were really excursions, the wind sidelong like a cool glance. My school desk would be empty, the blackboard full of fractions. The day, imagined, slipped past me, while the real day began in the kitchen and stayed there long into the afternoon: my mother and her cooking – her *preparation*, as she called it. She'd give me potatoes to peel and a short knife, guiding my hands until I had the feel of it. The peel flaked onto the table, never the continuous ribbon she was able to summon. Working the knife felt like learning a new word.

My mother spoke the physical language of cooking so well that it made me almost shy to attempt, yet she was patient. She wanted me to know. At least, to know these things. How to cook, how to launder. How to do the unseen tasks as thoroughly as if they were visible.

At the kitchen sink together, soaping the collars of shirts, I'd forget my life beyond the house. The sink was our small sea, a washday Wash of domestic proportion. We used a green brick of *Fairy* soap, and over the weeks it made a gradual mystery of letters that shrank away until the bar was just a lozenge. I loved its soapiness and its reticence, and the extravagance of cold water that my mother pulled from the tap to rinse it all away. A necessary plenty, she said of it. You had to move some water to wash a shirt clean.

I didn't appreciate then how much it meant to her to be able to make things look new, to wash the labour out of them and rinse away my father's fatigue. With him gone from us, this was something she could do to bring him near: if not the man, then his clothes in her arms. Her own fatigue at keeping things going alone, she wouldn't admit to. I came to understand what it might have meant to be a housewife, which is what my mother said she was. It was to love the house and its doings as truly as she loved my father.

When the green soap wore down to a sliver, I'd deposit it in a jar with other remnants. Later, my mother and I would melt them down and make a new bar of mongrel soap. Soap for the dog, she'd say, although the dog was never washed.

The record player looked like a suitcase. It was a portable Columbia my parents had brought back from Germany along with their real suitcases, years before I was born. I was fascinated by it and afraid of it – the records spinning without stopping if you didn't lower the arm, and the arm itself, like the arm of a mantis, its fly-leg stylus, and the explosive percussion if you dropped it on the vinyl. That the case was khaki coloured, the colour of soldiers, made it seem like regulation equipment, and as if the soldiering part of my father's life, of which he seldom spoke, might reappear, perhaps disguised as songs but in a code I could crack. One day my brother coaxed me to put on a record. He showed me how little of myself it took to lift and guide the arm – *Look, just a finger.*

A big, jangling ball of guitars came bouncing over us. Nothing the pinafored Von Trapps would sing. It was a loud, oily sound. My brother knew how to listen to it. Turn it down a bit, would you, please – my mother coming in with a frown against the noise. Turned down, it was the music of engines waiting to race, motorbikes, boys with long hair and lipstick revving the frets.

You didn't have to start at the beginning. You could aim for the space before the song you wanted to hear. The space gave you the whole song. He showed me how to see it, my eye level with the turntable, finding the black shine. There was a power in this; he had taught me the beginnings of taste. I began skipping over some tracks in favour of others: 'Wonderful World', 'Shall We Dance?' They weren't my records but they were my rehearsals – for what, I wasn't certain except that, in singing them, I loved their rhymes and tunes and the word *perchance*, which seemed such a grown-up word, such a luxurious way of saying *maybe*.

[play it again]

One year I miss almost a third of my schooling. I miss my friends. I also grow to like the time alone. When we all come down with measles, my friends and their mothers come to our house to play together, taking advantage of the collective illness. I feel myself pulled between two worlds. The friends aren't interested in listening to old LPs, and my mother doesn't put them on since we have company. Nor are they interested in peeling potatoes or melting down the soap. They come to the house with dolls whose arms and legs bend realistically, whose hard plastic waists are egg-timer slender. There we sit, three girls and a half-dozen dolls between us, our arms and faces speckled with rash, animating the still lives in our itching hands.

I'm relieved when they go, taking their dolls with them. The house resumes its usual music. Later that afternoon my father returns for the weekend. My brother comes in from his after school job. The evening hushes down and the wood pigeons hoot their laments. My brother tells me that they aren't sad birds; they just have voices that sound that way. *Damned woodpigeons*, my father calls them. They wake him up too early, and their dusk hoots are like a bad premonition. Yet, when I'm sick, if he is home, it is my father who comes to me from his scarce sleep and reads from a book. Stories are the source of soothing and falling. I don't know this as a thought, only as sensation – falling: words into my ears, me toward sleep, not caring how the story ends. It is the voice that matters. The voice is the story.

How did a person become an adult, beyond getting older, that is? This was my perpetual question as a child. The inscrutable world of manners, the separateness of work. My father in his shed with the cricket on the radio. My mother in her kitchen with her twenty pounds of plums. The things you said or didn't say, and the knowing when and to whom to say them. I couldn't fathom it: being taller, being alone, being together. The pairing off, like the Ark, the two-by-two. How did it happen?

In the stack of LPs there was a record sleeve with a man and woman on the beach, lying in the waves. It could have been Holme beach or Thornham. It would be like that. You needed scenery to fall in love. It seemed accidental, the place deciding when it would happen – a beach so lonely that you had to throw yourself upon it with another person.

My mother stayed somewhere in the middle of her work, while the records spun toward their last notes on the turntable. The pocket calendar she kept in her purse flagged Sunday as the week's beginning, but really the week began in kitchens on a wash day, and always had. Sunday was a last day, my father's departure back to London and beyond. It was also a place we went to – a church, a beach, a drive through the back roads before he left – a *from which*, from which we'd return to the house, which was eternal. Laundry was, cooking was, my mother's way of handling eternity.

And then there was Dennis Brain. Listen to this, my father would say. It was a Saturday, always a Saturday, the weekend ahead of him, and he'd put the record on and start to mend a fuse box or a fishing line. This is music, he'd say. This is the sort of music you will never forget. Mozart wrote it and no one plays it better than Dennis. (*Dennis*, as if he was a friend.) I'd file it away in my memory, the horn's shining tune and the happiness it brought my father to hear it. It stayed long in his mind after the weekend. He'd whistle bits of it unexpectedly when next he came home. It was a kind of love that asked nothing of him.

Really, all of it was *preparation*, or, I might say now, prelude, for my mother's housework and my father's absences made a duet alongside the other songs. I learned to sing it, too. By the time I was a young woman heading into the 1990s, their music was a miscued soundtrack for the complicated restlessness I found there. When love finally showed up it was heading for the city, skint and fickle. I did my best to cook it a good dinner.

[liner notes]

1. Charmian Carr plays Liesl Von Trapp singing 'Sixteen Going on Seventeen' in the 1965 film *The Sound of Music*.

2. The Von Trapps sing 'So Long, Farewell' as they make their escape from the Nazis.

3. Oklahoma! Broadway musical 1943, film 1955.

4. South Pacific, Broadway musical 1949, film 1958.

5. Ella Fitzgerald sings Irving Berlin's 'Blue Skies' on her 1959 album *Get Happy!*

6. Charles Aznavour's hit song 'In the Old Fashioned Way' spends 15 weeks on the British charts in 1973.

7. In *The Wizard of Oz*, Dorothy, played by Judy Garland, clicks the heels of her ruby slippers three times, saying 'There's no place like home...' to return home.

8. In the original stage version of *South Pacific*, Nellie Forbush, played by Mary Martin, performs 'I'm Gonna Wash That Man Right Outa My Hair'. In 1980, Clairol repurpose the song to advertise hair dye.

9. T-Rex's 'Metal Guru', by Marc Bolan, tops British charts for four weeks in 1972 and appears on the album *The Slider.* Bolan dies in a car accident in 1977.

10. Louis Armstrong releases the hit single 'What a Wonderful World', written by Thiele and Weiss, in 1967.

11. Deborah Kerr and Yul Brynner duet in 'Shall We Dance' in the 1956 film *The King and I.* The word 'perchance' appears in this song.

12. Deborah Kerr and Burt Lancaster share the iconic tidal kiss in the 1953 film *From Here to Eternity.*

13. Dennis Brain performs Mozart Horn Concertos 1-4 with the Philharmonia Orchestra and Herbert von Karajan on the Columbia label, 1953. Brain dies in a car accident in 1957.

Acknowledgements

My gratitude for Richard Rogers and Oscar Hammerstein II, whose brilliant songs were my first experience of art; for the Google searches, YouTube views, and Wikipedia notes that helped me get the dates right; and for my family's record collection for memories and inspiration.

Liner notes 5,6,8,9,10 draw upon information from the following hyperlinks:

Get Happy! (Ella Fitzgerald album), http://en.wikipedia.org/w/index.php?title=Get_Happy!_(Ella_Fitzgerald_album)&oldid=578134488 (last visited Feb. 1, 2014).

The Old Fashioned Way (song), http://en.wikipedia.org/w/index.php?title=The_Old_Fashioned_Way_(song)&oldid=553509484 (last visited Feb. 1, 2014). I'm Gonna Wash That Man Right Outa My Hair, http://en.wikipedia.org/w/index.php?title=I%27m_Gonna_Wash_That_Man_Right_Outa_My_Hair&oldid=584775378 (last visited Feb. 1, 2014).

Metal Guru, http://en.wikipedia.org/w/index.php?title=Metal_Guru&oldid=588198021 (last visited Feb. 1, 2014).

What a Wonderful World, http://en.wikipedia.org/w/index.php?title=What_a_Wonderful_World&oldid=593014340 (last visited Feb. 1, 2014).

Taken For Granted

- Layn Feldman -

One Wednesday evening Betty phoned her sister Rose.

Rifka Goldblatt died she said.

Rifka Goldblatt? said Rose.

Rifka Goldblatt said Betty.

She can't be dead said Rose.

Why not? asked Betty.

Because said Rose, this is the woman who reckoned that the way to live a very long life was to always be a little bit ill. I've followed her advice ever since.

And it shows. So, how'd you think she died?

How many guesses do I get?

None said Betty. She was killed in Blumleins, when a rival baker tried to steal Danny's recipe for his egg cholla. Rifka got caught in the cross fire.

Danny Blumlein has a gun?

I never mentioned a gun.

So where was the cross fire?

They were throwing whatever came to hand. The rival bakers had brought along stale beigals as ammunition and Danny and his people retaliated with macaroons. After Pesach, who chooses to eat macaroons?

That's what killed Rifka?

No, she just caught one on the side of the head, which stunned her. It was falling on the stone floor what killed her.

Why do I not believe you?

Because I made it all up. Not bad I thought.

Rose sighed. This could only mean one thing. You're going to that writing class, aren't you?

I felt like joining something.

How about the human race? Is Rifka Goldblatt dead or not?

Oh she's dead.

And how did she die?

In her sleep last night.

Wait a minute. She lives alone since her Herbie died, who found her?

Why does it matter?

Because said Rose, if you live alone, there's gotta be somebody with a key to find you, because if not, you could be dead for months until the overpowering smell causes the neighbours, who never thought to come and check on you, to complain to the council. Oh Please God I don't die in my bath, I would die of embarrassment to be found naked in a cold bath.

You'd be dead, why would you care?

I would care. You've got my door key, so from now on I want you to phone me every morning and every evening without fail. That way, if I don't answer you'll know I would've died and you can get round here before I start to go off. And, if God forbid I should've died in my bath, you can get me dried off and dressed appropriately. I'll write you out a list of what clothes I want to wear, how to do my hair and of course, there's my make-up.

What about me? said Betty.

Same rule can apply, though I'd have to get a cab to get over to you, and after a certain time at night, they charge double.

I'll make sure I die during daylight hours said Betty.

Thank you. So, who did find her?

Her sister Lila was coming over for a visit.

See! Rifka must've given Lila a key in case what happened happened.

No said Betty. Lila just knew how to pick a lock. Rifka once told my friend Sylvie, that her sister was a member of Mossad.

You mean said Rose, we once knew somebody who had a sister who was in the secret service?

Wha'd'yer know.

This of course means said Rose, that Rifka knew when her sister would be arriving, and it follows that she knew if she died on Tuesday night, there'd be somebody to find her soon after…

Are you suggesting that Rifka arranged to die when she did?

Could be. Much more considerate than Doris Popoff's mother dying while Doris was on holiday in Rimini.

Definitely.

If Rifka died last night, does it count that she died on the Tuesday, or would it be counted as a Wednesday?

Why?

Because I'd like to know how much time I've got to decide what to wear for the lavoyah.

If it's tomorrow then I better get a move on, but if it's Friday, then you can take us to Brent Cross for me to find something else. I think I've still got a nice black hat somewhere…

Oooh breathed Betty, I like the way you immediately assume I'm going to drive you…

But if the lavoyah is on Friday argued Rose, then Thursday is our usual day for going to Brent Cross to have a look around anyway. This Thursday we would really have something to look for.

Sometimes said Betty, trying to control her temper, I can't believe how you take me for granted!

Of course I do. On the one hand I know that you'll always be there for me. On the other hand, you know that I know you'll always be there for me. Works both ways. How did you find out about Rifka?

Shlomo Hugerman told us.

Us who? And why would Shlomo know?

This is what you miss when you don't come to shul. I keep telling you, but you don't listen. Shlomo was with Rifka on the football committee. They were having a thing. He looked terrible today when he came to tell us.

But Rifka must've been in her eighties, and Shlomo always looked like he was thinking of going somewhere but couldn't remember where.

So?

No, you're right said Rose. I think it's a good thing when somebody dies that those who professed to love the person who just died, look terrible. This is what I kept telling my mirror after my Arty evashalom died. I just thought: I must've loved him to look this bad. You looked pretty awful when your Frank died.

Thank you. Will you look terrible when I die?

Who says you're going first? I'm older, you should be the one looking terrible.

Then who's going to look terrible for me?

Rose couldn't answer so she side stepped. Who can you phone to find out whether the lavoyah is tomorrow or Friday? she asked.

Why don't you phone? said Betty.

Fine said Rose. Just tell me who.

Betty thought for a bit. Lila you can phone. She's staying at Rifka's house to sort things out.

Rose phoned Lila.

Hello said a voice.

Is that Lila?

Who wants to know?

I was a friend of your sister Rifka.

Your name please.

My name is Rose Goldman.

I never heard this name before.

How about BettyTefel?

You said your name was Rose Goldman, now you want to change it.

No no no. My sister is Betty Tefel, maybe that name is familiar to you?

Tefel? Any relation to Frank Tefel?

Why do you ask?

Why are you asking when I'm already asking?

I'm just wondering how you would know Frank Tefel.

Who said I know him?

Knew him. Frank died some years ago. He was Betty's husband, my brother-in-law.

Frank died?

Yes.

But that's terrible. Oh. Lovely man Frank.

Yes. So you knew him.

Frank Tefel died? But he was a young man.

Maybe when you knew him…

The lavoyah for my sister is on Friday said Lila. We'll set off from here at 11.30 hours. Come before if you want a cup of tea. I think it will be cold.

And with that she put the phone down.

*

Thursday turned out to be great fun for both sisters. Rose bought Betty a rather fetching hat, and treated herself to a pair of shoes which Betty thought were totally unsuitable for a funeral, being bright red patent stilettos, but decided it best to keep shtum and patted her hat box, knowing her cat Jaffa would love to curl up in it.

Rose decided not to tell Betty about Lila knowing her Frank, though in what sense Lila had known Frank was still a mystery.

*

Come Friday morning quite a crowd gathered at Rifka's house.

Sylvie came round with cups of tea for the women, whilst whisky had been laid on for the men. Betty asked if Lila would be sitting shiva, and Sylvie said No, she had to fly out before shabbas came in, but Shlomo had extended an invitation to anyone who cared to come back to his flat afterwards.

*

As they all stood in the small cold hall for prayers, Betty was still wondering who would look terrible for her when she died. She had a pretty good idea that her friend Sylvie would be somewhat upset, but looking terrible? Betty wasn't so sure.

Someone in the congregation began to sob, and Rose was surprised to see a rather chubby woman in glasses with mousy hair pull out a large handkerchief and blow her nose loudly. That was Lila, Betty thought, had to be.

Rose knew at once that the mousy woman couldn't be Lila. Anybody she reckoned, who'd been in Mossad would be that hard to withstand any amount of despair and sadness.

Then all too soon it was time to follow behind the coffin, carried on a simple cart to the grave site.

*

Afterwards Betty and Rose walked over to their husbands.

Rose brushed the dirt from Arty's stone, removed the weeds from around the grave, and left a small pebble to show she'd visited. She looked over to where Betty stood, running her hand over the engraving on her Frank's stone.

Rose would've liked to have gone over and asked Frank how he knew Lila, but unlike her Arty, Frank Tefel was never much of a talker.

The two sisters walked slowly back to the car.

I was right about Lila said Betty, as she fastened her seat belt.

About what? asked Rose.

About the woman in the glasses crying with the big handkerchief. That was Lila.

Never said Rose.

But it was said Betty, I asked Shlomo, and he confirmed it for me.

Of course said Rose. Very clever.

How so?

I imagined that any woman in Mossad must look hard, when a real spy would use as her cover a round mousy looking woman in glasses, who you'd never suspect.

I thought it was her.

No you didn't.

Yes I did said Betty, because I recognised her from somewhere, but I can't for the life of me remember when and how I would've met her.

Rose jumped in before she had time to think – D'yer think maybe Frank knew her?

In what way? asked Betty. Why would Frank know her?

Well, began Rose… He was a tailor…

So…? Betty didn't like where this was going. Why would you

think my Frank ever knew Lila?

Well Lila knew Frank said Rose, she told me.

But you didn't think to tell me said Betty.

I was trying to pick a good time to tell you.

And you think straight after we bury a friend is a good time.

Why you getting broygus with me?

Because I know you said Betty, and I can see where this is going. You immediately jumped to the conclusion that there'd been something going on between my Frank and Lila. Why bother to ask me if Frank knew her, when you knew already that Frank knew her.

I just wondered how she knew him.

You mean how well she knew him said Betty.

And now she felt angry. What right had Rose to say such things that she must know would upset her.

Betty stopped the car.

Get out, she said.

What?

I don't want to be in the same car as you said Betty. Tucka, driving somebody who seems to enjoy upsetting me. Get out of my car.

But we're nowhere near Shlomo's flat said Rose. How am I supposed to get there?

I don't know said Betty, and I don't care.

Fine! said Rose, struggling to unfasten the seat belt and get out of the car as angrily as she could muster.

Betty drove off.

She kept her eyes on the road, still angry, but desperately trying to remember when she'd met Lila before... She'd recognised her from somewhere.

But from where, and how many years ago?

What if she'd never met Lila, and it was just that she reminded Betty of somebody. But if that was the case, then Frank knew Lila without ever introducing her to Betty.

When she got to Shlomo's flat everybody asked her where Rose was, but Betty just shrugged. Sylvie made a face though.

So what's with you and Rose now? she asked.

I don't want to talk about my sister right now said Betty, except to say that she can be a very unkind hurtful person who only thinks about herself.

And it's taken you all these years to figure that one out? said Sylvie.

Betty looked at her friend. I am allowed to hate her sometimes she said.

Of course you are said Sylvie, she's big enough to take it.

Oh she is that said Betty, and they both laughed.

Still, thought Betty, Rose was right about one thing. Shlomo did look terrible enough to have really cared about Rifka. He looked so lost in that suit he was wearing, as though he'd shrunk over night. Shame, because she could tell it'd been made by a somebody who knew his craft...

Tailor made.

Frank was a tailor.

Tailors made suits. Frank was a bespoke tailor...

Sometimes he took on private jobs, and Betty would help out on her sewing machine...

She recalled a woman who came to the house quite late at night because Frank said it was the only time she could get there. Betty remembered opening the door of an evening and letting her in to see Frank... because Frank was making a jacket for her.

That was Lila!

It was OK. Everything was OK. She took a slice of Sylvie's delicious yeast cake and another cup of tea.

She was still angry with Rose, but that was OK as well.

*

However, she worried over Rose a bit when she got home.

Walking in those shoes couldn't have been easy, and what was she supposed to do about ringing her sister every evening to make sure she was still alive...

Jaffa was sitting atop the kitchen stool, waiting to see what he was going to be offered for dinner.

Should she phone Rose? God forbid something had happened and Betty's last words to her sister had been Get out of my car! Her hand hovered over the pouch with tuna and salmon. But hadn't she given Jaffa tuna and salmon in the morning? She pulled out the pouch with lamb.

The phone rang and she jumped.

It was Rose.

I thought you might like to know she began, that I'm still alive with no thanks to you and I managed to get a cab home. At least Jack Walker still loves me… Dogs are always dependable like that she said and put the phone down.

Betty rang back.

I still love you she told her sister, and put the phone down.

Did she?

She looked down at Jaffa, who was still waiting to be fed.

Course I do she thought.

The phone rang again.

It was Rose

I know what this is all about she said. This is your way of showing me that I shouldn't take you for granted. That's why you pushed me out of your car. It took me a while to get it, but now I got it.

No said Betty. You haven't got it. I didn't push you out of my car, I just told you to get out – There was no pushing.

Maybe you didn't physically shove me out of the car, but you as good as did.

Betty wanted this over with as quickly as possible, but with Rose making it harder, which meant it would take longer, it was all beginning to make Betty feel more and more angry. Jaffa was sitting there, with his eyes moving from the pouch to Betty and back to the pouch.

I will make this very brief she said, trying to control her voice. I was angry at you firstly because Lila told you she knew my Frank and you didn't tell me. Secondly because you then assumed there must've been something going on between them, and… She knew there must be another thing that drove her mad about her sister… And it didn't even bother you that there'd be no body there to be feel terrible when I died! Now Jaffa has been waiting long enough to be fed, so that's what I'm going to do.

Whereupon she slammed the phone down, and went off to feed her cat.

Half an hour later Rose rang Betty.

What I forgot to say is how you can't take anything for granted. Look how I thought Arty would be around for ever. Maybe I like to know you will feel terrible when I die, because you are the one person I can take for granted will feel terrible, whereas I know that when you die there will be a lot more people looking terrible. And who knows, if you're lucky, maybe you'll die before me, and then I will get to feel terrible.

Is this your way of apologising? asked Betty.

No said Rose, because as far as I'm concerned I have nothing to apologise for.

Nothing?

I don't do sorry.

Well maybe you should.

I think you've got more to apologise for than I have.

Like what?

Like pushing me out of the car when I was wearing shoes that weren't suitable for walking so far in.

Well you shouldn't have been wearing such stupid shoes in the first place, and you said you got a cab so there wasn't that much walking anyway. AND!, she shouted, AND, FOR THE LAST TIME – I DID NOT PUSH YOU OUT OF THE CAR!

YES YOU DID! shouted Rose and put the phone down.

Betty rang her sister back.

No I didn't, she said very quietly, and quickly put the phone down before Rose could say anything in return.

Rose put her phone down. This is not finished, she told Jack Walker. And she was right.

A Time For Rain

- C.G. Menon -

'Is an elephant bigger than a shark, Dada? How about *two* elephants?'

It's the latest craze at his school, and my grandson is wearing out his tongue with questions. Little Arjun wants to know whether trains are faster than cheetahs, or whales are longer than buses, or monkeys are smarter than dogs.

'Why do you have to compare?' I ask him. 'Can't things just be themselves?'

But perhaps it's in the blood, these comparisons. Because seventy years ago in a village in Malaya, I learnt that love is as heavy as 159 mangoes.

Let me explain.

I grew up in Pahang, the sprawling centre of Malaysia, and the last of its states to be overrun by cities. The palm trees jostled close around our *kampong*, the crickets marched into our ears on a thousand tinny notes, and under massy tropical clouds the ocean waters – the only ones I'd ever seen – writhed with sea snakes.

Seventy years ago, I was a grubby boy, snake-thin and cricket-loud, running barefoot from school through the mud of the forest trails, sucking frozen *ais kacang* till my mouth was as scarlet as the parrots flashing overhead.

My mother would scold me, 'Sunil! Throw away those filthy sweets before you get sick; you don't know where the man gets his water from.'

But that day, *the* day, she cuffed my head in exasperation as I rushed past. 'Put on a *baju* before going out to play! The monsoons have brought mosquitoes already.'

She had an almost superstitious belief in the power of a *baju* – nothing more than a thin cotton shirt – to prevent mosquito bites, even though I noisily complained that it did nothing but make me hot. But long ago she had lost two sisters to malaria, a disease that snatched the young in those days. Little bright-eyed, dusky, coltish ghosts, my dead aunts clattered about our home, ate the sweets we left at the door for them, and twisted our carefully laid-out clothes into elaborate knots each night. In Malaya the dead are curious, they come back – and when more likely than at the monsoon, when everything is alive?

But I was twelve, and a hero amongst men and had no time for any of that. I could sense the upcoming rain in the way the damp air slid across my skin; in the way the geckos scrawled their secrets in a lacing dance across the walls and the curlews screamed from silver skies. I wanted to spend one last evening with Chetan – my schoolmate since babyhood – before the downpour that would halt our play for weeks.

Chetan met me at the door as I was reluctantly pulling my old cotton *baju* over my head.

'Sunil, you old reprobate. Don't waste time getting dressed in your best!' Chetan was dramatic; a posturing, languishing actor of the old school. Each year, our teacher would relive her own faded dreams by giving him increasingly elegant speeches and words to memorise. The quaint syllables sounded carefully in his mouth, rounded and cool like pebbles underwater.

'Quickly, I have an hour before dinner. What will we do?' I always followed Chetan's lead, fitting my steps into his footprints as we walked. But that evening he pulled me close as we ran down the street, his mouth twitching with a suppressed secret.

'Uncle Apan is working at the temple,' he burst out. 'Let's go and spy!' Chetan's Uncle Apan, our majestically stern headmaster, also acted as the sole priest at our remote Hindu temple. Because there were so few visitors Apan's position had been nominal only, and the temple had fallen into disuse long ago. It crouched beyond the boundaries of civilisation, out on the frontier where the *kampong* fought the jungle. The track to it was overgrown and our parents had sternly forbidden us from playing there because of its isolation and dangerously crumbling walls. This made no difference to us, of course, and we had long ago explored the bare yard and daringly scribbled graffiti over the blurred carvings. But this was the first time in years that the temple itself had been opened, an event reserved only for those pilgrims who offered a sizeable donation. It promised a breathless adventure before dark, before the days of rain.

'Yes! Come on, slowcoach.' Pulling Chetan by the hand, I scrambled up a crumbling bank of clay by the roadside. 'We need to disguise ourselves so we can spy.'

I pulled off the hated *baju* – what spy would bother about mosquitoes! – and slapped handfuls of mud on my face. 'We'll be Red Indians.'

'I'm Geronimo,' Chetan claimed hastily. 'And you can be...' – looking into the skies for inspiration – 'Rain Storm Coming.'

Splashing mud like seawater, we raced down the path that led to the temple, shooing squawking chickens and wayward goats aside with our war-whoops.

'I bet it's a thief!' I gasped excitedly as we scrambled off the path. 'He wants Apan to forgive him, but first he has to beg penance in sackcloth and ashes.'

'Or a... a millionaire.' Chetan's thoughts always took a more definite cast than my romantic wanderings. 'And he's so pleased with the temple that he gives us all a million *ringgit*. And we can all own cars and horses, and live in palaces, and – '

He stopped abruptly, holding a hand up for silence in a signal we'd learnt from our tattered Boys' Own magazines. I could hear voices, and I pushed forward to see, the two of us elbowing each other in a silent squabble as we jostled to peer past a tangle of fibrous banyan roots.

Apan stood with his back to us before a giant set of weighing scales, dragged out of their usual service at the markets. Each scale pan was large enough to hold several sacks of rice, a heaped mound of taro, or once – most memorably – a pair of struggling young goats. He was addressing an unknown listener behind the temple wall.

'You must fulfill your prayers to Lord Vishnu,' he intoned sonorously. 'When your infant daughter was ill with typhoid you pledged her weight in fruit and honey as a gift if she survived.' Apan had a strong, resonant voice and it was clear where Chetan had inherited his taste for fine phrases.

'Just like the Aga Khan!' I whispered excitedly behind our screen. Last year we had scavenged my mother's old newspapers from a drawer, and had re-enacted over and over again the Jubilee celebration where the Aga Khan – Chetan, by demand – had given his own weight in gold to the poor, played resentfully by me.

'Except it's a baby, not a prince,' retorted Chetan in a disgusted voice. 'They're going to give Apan a few sacks of fruit and just go again. There's no gold, or thief, or… or anything!' His disappointment was contagious; certainly the exchange of a few bananas over a crying baby was a poor end to our spying game.

But then Apan moved aside and, stepping out from the temple walls, I saw a girl. Perhaps a year younger than me, she was shepherded anxiously from behind by her parents and was looking about her with complete self-possession. She blinked in the flat copper glare of the sinking sun, and each downward beat of her eyelashes echoed a strangely choked beat of my heart.

'I'm Sushila,' she volunteered boldly, resting her eyes on Apan for a moment. It seemed to me that she was seeing through him, past him, to where I knelt. Her voice was only for me, for the two of us alone on this hillside of evening flowers on the brink of the rains.

'Climb on the scales, child. Hurry; before it gets dark.' Apan shook his head reprovingly at her parents. 'Ten years you delayed, and now you come a day before the monsoon!'

Sushila giggled and her laugh surged deep in my belly. She was wearing a faded yellow top that had perhaps once been gold, with a rust-brown skirt stained with dust about her knees. Before this I had been careful to imitate Chetan's loud disdain for the village girls, but now her gold and brown image was sweeping my world away.

'They don't want to wait any more in case I get bigger,' she confided to Apan, settling comfortably onto the scale pan as her mother fluttered about with murmured apologies. Her father resignedly began to heap mangos on the other side, taking handfuls from a sack slung over the back of a tired and patient bullock he had coaxed into the yard. Each mango tumbled heavily onto the weight poised against Sushila as she squatted there like a butterfly after rain. Slowly, softly… 120, 150, 159 fruits in a heap of sunset gold. And then some broken combs of honey tossed haphazardly on the top, spilling droplets which trickled like the dampness on her neck. And Sushila was laughing all the time, a witch's call in my ear. She was plunging her hands deep into the soft pile of mangos, snatching a honeycomb to break into shivered fragments and crushing them between her sharp white teeth…

And then it was over. Apan had again blocked our view and Sushila was gone, leaving the clearing empty of everything but the clopping of a bullock's hooves, a tattered pair of market scales, and a pile of overripe fruit.

'Come on, Sunil!' Chetan impatiently ordered. 'Maybe Apan will let us into the temple at least.'

But how could we pretend to be spies now, with so much more than I had bargained for? I refused to play any more, and we almost quarrelled. And all I remember of that day besides is that the rains came next morning, blotting out from its history all but the image of a gold and brown girl, and the beating of my heart.

So much has changed, in a lifetime. Chetan left the village some years later for an English university, and for all I know became the millionaire he'd always yearned to be. My mother died with a secret on her lips, slipping away to join the exuberant ghosts of her sisters. Each year the jungle encroached further on the temple yard, until there was nothing but glinting gold statues of Shiva and the crumbling dust of incense sticks to show there had ever been anything there. And – because this is not a sad story, you see – I moved away too, crossed oceans I'd never seen before, met and married a girl whose image also swept my world away.

But years later – and how enchanting, how absurd to be learning how many years fill a lifetime – some things remain. And so I stand in the stark light of a supermarket, reaching out a strangely wrinkled hand to sterile mangoes packaged in cold storage for most of their lives. And I still weigh each handful against love, against the weight of fruit and honey and heartbreak.

Happy Families

- Karen O'Connor -

'Wakey, wakey.'

Isla struggled through the deep fog of sleep as she tried to recognise the voice that called her awake. 'Rise and shine.' The voice was female and had a gentle sing song quality.

'Mum?' The word came out as a strangled gurgle.

'Give yourself a minute little one.' The face of a plump, middle aged woman came into Isla's view. 'I believe those first few seconds can be uncomfortable.'

'What?' Isla took a small breath and winced as air grated down her throat.

'It's pardon.' The woman frowned down at her.

Isla looked around. She was lying down, so could only get a view of the plain, white ceiling, air conditioning vents and the top of the woman's head who was sitting next to her.

'Who are you?' Isla asked.

'My name is Miss Brownlee.'

'Am I in hospital?'

'You're in Adoption Centre Number Six.' Miss Brownlee gave a small smile before smoothing her mousy hair.

'What?'

'No, dear, it's pardon.' Miss Brownlee sighed. 'Maybe I made a mistake choosing to see you. You looked so sweet in your hologram.'

'No, I mean what's an adoption centre?' Isla tried to sit up but her body didn't want to cooperate.

'Oh! Don't tell me they haven't inducted you?' She leaned forward and touched Isla's face.

'Induction into what?'

'This is terrible. You hear of such stories in the news. Children taken in and abandoned without being told they're on the adoption list.'

'Why was I taken?' Isla's voice trembled.

'Let me check the information.' Miss Brownlee disappeared, returning with a palm pad. 'Isla Edwards. That's a pretty name. You were adopted in the year twenty two thirty three. You were aged ten when you came here.'

'How old am I now?' Isla struggled to remember what the date was.

'You're still ten you silly thing.'

'What?'

Miss Brownlee's mouth tightened. 'You really don't have very good manners.'

'Sorry.' Isla cleared her throat. 'Could you tell me how long I've been here?'

Miss Brownlee looked down at the palm pad. 'Eighty two years.'

Isla closed her eyes for a few seconds as her sluggish brain added the figures together. 'I'm ninety two!'

'Oh dear, you really haven't been told anything about this process.'

'Can *you* tell me what's going on?'

'I can't afford to spend my money on doing your induction.'

Isla frowned. 'You're paying to see me?'

'That's what we have to do these days, ever since the babies stopped coming.' Miss Brownlee patted her stomach. 'If we want children we come to an adoption centre like this. I've never wanted a tiny baby, but a child of about your age sounded just right.'

Isla tried to process this information. 'Is my brother here?' she finally asked, wondering what had happened to Artemus, her younger brother.

'I'm not interested in little boys. I don't want to waste my money on seeing their grubby faces.' Miss Brownlee sniffed and straightened her skirt over thick, grey knitted tights.

'Did my parents give me up?'

Miss Brownlee's forehead crinkled. 'I'm not made of money. If I go over my five minutes I have to pay again.'

'Please,' Isla said.

Miss Brownlee glanced at her watch and then studied the palm pad. 'It looks like you all contracted Kennedy's Disease. Most likely your parents put you in here in the hope of a cure being found.'

'Is there a cure?' Isla had never heard of Kennedy's Disease.

'Sorry, my time's up.' Miss Brownlee pressed a button by the side of Isla's bed.

'You are as cute as a button.'

Isla blinked herself awake. A tall, thin man stood over her, leaning so close she could feel his breath on her cheek.

'Hello little lady, I'm Mr Gibson.'

'Hello, sir.' Isla remembered her manners this time.

'Adorable.' Mr Gibson sat down close to Isla. 'You are just what I've been looking for.'

'May I ask what year it is?'

'It's the year twenty two fifty two.'

'I've been here a long time,' Isla said more to herself than her new visitor.

'Which is one of the reasons I decided to visit you.'

'Why?'

'The children that have been here the longest tend to be cheaper.' He picked some lint from his faded suit jacket. 'There's a higher risk of cellular breakdown if you've been here over fifty years.'

Isla shook her head. She didn't like the sound of cellular breakdown.

'Don't look so worried my little cutey. Give your new daddy a smile.'

Isla obliged, but couldn't avoid squirming under Mr Gibson's intense stare.

'Did you have to pay to see me?' Isla remembered the last woman she had spoken to, complaining about the cost.

'I pay to visit all the children I like to look of. Then we get to spend some time together and if we're a good match I buy you.'

'What about my illness?'

'I pay to revive you and cure your illness.' Mr Gibson smiled down at her. 'That is, of course, if I think we're well suited.'

'I have Kennedy's Disease.' Isla tried to figure out what he meant by reviving her.

'I know, but that's curable now, although not all that cheap. It's a good job you're such a pretty little thing.'

'Can you help me get out of bed?' Isla tried to stretch. 'I feel like I haven't moved in forever.'

Mr Gibson laughed. 'You can't move.'

'Because of the illness?'

'Only your head is reanimated.'

Isla tried to lift her legs. 'Nothing's happening.' She struggled to make her limbs work, but the only thing that moved was her head, which twisted side to side as she willed movement into her body.

'You won't be able to move. The Centre believes it's too risky to reanimate your whole body each time you get a visitor. Not to mention the cost involved and the possibility of you escaping and spreading your illness.'

'Will you get me out of here?' Isla tried to quell the fear inside her at the realisation she was trapped.

Mr Gibson paused. 'What will you do if I pay for you to come home with me?'

'You want to adopt me, right? I'd be a good daughter. The best daughter you'll ever have.'

Mr Gibson's eyes glistened and perspiration dotted his top lip. 'I like good girls.'

'My parents thought I was good.'

'Children your age are just perfect. Still young, with an air of innocence, but you know how the world really works.' Mr Gibson leaned forward and slowly ran a strand of Isla's hair through his fingers. Isla instinctively moved her head to the side, away from Mr Gibson's sweaty palm.

'Don't flinch from me.' Mr Gibson's fingers tightened in Isla's hair and he pulled her head back towards him.

'Maybe I'm not such a good girl after all,' she whispered, just before the lights went out.

'Hello, my girl.' A finger tapped Isla's cheek. She opened her eyes, hoping that it wasn't Mr Gibson. A round, jolly faced woman stared back at her.

'Do you speak?' she asked, after a few seconds spent studying Isla's face.

'Yes, ma'am.'

'I had a sister called Isla. When I saw your name on the list I just had to visit.' The woman smiled and rested her hands in her lap. 'I'm Violet Madison.'

'Hello, Mrs Madison. It's a pleasure to meet you.'

'It's Miss Madison. I never married, there didn't seem much point in having a man around when they lost the ability to give us girls, babies.'

Isla tried to smile but her lips were too dry to move.

'Oh, you poor thing. You look like you're wearing out.' Miss Madison leaned forward and wiped something across Isla's lips. 'It's just lip balm but it will help with your chapped skin. I sometimes wonder just how good these facilities are. They don't seem to have taken much care of you.'

'I think I've been here a long time,' said Isla. She smacked her lips together, enjoying the sticky, cherry scented balm.

'You have,' said Miss Madison. 'Which is another reason I thought you might like a visitor.'

'Thank you.' From her prone position, Isla looked Miss Madison over. 'Are you thinking of adopting me?'

'Yes, I am. I have a room at home, made up for a little girl. I've had it ready for ten years, so the toys might be a bit out of date by now.'

'It sounds nice.'

'I've always wanted a child of my own. I've been saving for such a long time to come here and meet you all.'

Isla swallowed. 'Are there lots of other children here?'

Miss Madison laughed. 'Well, there's about ten thousand in this facility. You're on a floor that must have about five hundred other children.'

Isla's hopes plummeted. She hadn't realised how desperate she'd been to get out of what felt like a permanent death bed until now.

'Oh, don't fret child, I think you're lovely.' Miss Madison crouched down by Isla's side. 'To be honest I've always had a soft spot for the lost causes, and you seem pretty lost to me.'

Isla tried another smile, but her bottom lip wobbled, threatening a frown. Miss Madison placed a finger under Isla's chin and lifted it gently.

'I know this must be upsetting, but please believe me I'm here to help you if I can.'

'I hope you can.' The words came out as a squeak.

'Now, tell me about your childhood.' Miss Madison sat back down and gave Isla an encouraging smile.

Isla's brain scrambled as she delved for suitable memories. 'I have a brother.'

'Were you close?'

'He's my little brother, I used to look out for him.' Isla smiled. 'I used to take him hunting for crickets in the tiny patch of grass near our house.'

'What was he called?'

Isla paused. The way Miss Madison was talking made her wonder if her brother was dead. 'Artemus. I call him Arty for short.'

Miss Madison rubbed her chin with her thumb. 'Artemus, that rings a bell.'

'Have you seen him?'

'No, but it's the name, it's so unusual. I'm sure I've seen it on the adoption list on this floor.'

'He's here?' Isla would have jumped out of bed and hugged Miss Madison if only she could move.

'I haven't seen him. I don't really want a boy, but it's not unusual to keep family members in the same facility.'

'Do you think my parents are here too?' Isla's eyes lit up at the possibility of seeing her family.

'Let me check your records.' Miss Madison disappeared from Isla's view. 'No, it's recorded on your information log that they died of Kennedy's Disease. The cure's only been available for the last fifty years.'

Isla blinked back tears. 'My parents are dead.'

Miss Madison patted her cheek. 'Perhaps we could make a new family together.'

'With Arty? He's no trouble, in fact he's an angel,' Isla said, ignoring the memory in which Arty cut off one of her pig tails and threw it in a pond.

'Well, he sounds lovely, but I'm not interested in him.'

'Do you think I'm good enough for you?' Isla asked, biting hard on her bottom lip.

Miss Madison gave a small nod. 'Let me come back again and we can get to know each other better.'

'It's been really nice meeting you, Miss Madison.'

'Next time, you could try calling me Mum,' said Miss Madison as she shut Isla down.

Miss Madison came to visit Isla several more times. Isla couldn't resist the growing feelings of fondness she was developing for her. Miss Madison was her only contact to any kind of life and Isla found herself clinging to the moments they spent together.

'This is my fifth visit to see you,' Miss Madison said, as she finished braiding Isla's hair.

'Do you like me enough to take me home, Mum?'

'It's a little tricky.' Miss Madison coughed. 'You won't be aware of this, but there's been a bit of a hiccup in the economy.'

'But you've been saving haven't you?'

'I had all my savings in one bank, which is currently in liquidation.' Miss Madison blushed.

'I don't know what that means?'

'It means all of my money has gone, for now.' Miss Madison stroked Isla's forehead. 'I so wanted to take you home.'

'But you can't.' Isla closed her eyes for a few seconds.

'Don't be cross with me.'

'I'm not, I'm... sad.'

'I will get my money back one day and then I'll return for you.'

Isla kept her eyes shut. 'If you can't take me now, can you answer a question for me?'

'I'll do my very best,' said Miss Madison.

'My brother, Arty. Can you see if he's still here?'

'That should be easy. I'll check the list of names on the adoption inventory.'

Isla opened her eyes and watched as Miss Madison scrolled her finger down a palm pad.

'Artemus Edwards. Aged seven. He has Kennedy's Disease. Is that him?'

'Yes.' Isla breathed out slowly. All the time she'd been lying here and her baby brother was so close. She did have some family left after all.

'Has that made you happy?' Miss Madison asked.

Isla nodded. 'Thanks, Mum.'

'I'm turning you off now little one.'

'Just one more ask.'

Miss Madison gave her an indulgent smile. 'Just one.'

'If you ever get your money back would you consider buying Arty instead of me?'

Miss Madison blinked rapidly several times. 'Oh, I don't think so. He's a stranger to me, I want you.'

'Please, Mum, it would make me so happy to know my little brother was safe and well and being cared for by someone as nice as you.'

Miss Madison paused. 'For a child you can seem very grown up at times.'

'Is that a yes?' Isla's eyes kept straying to the life support switch, knowing her time was running out.

'I'll think about it. Sleep well child.'

Isla woke, convinced somebody had just said her name.

'Miss Madison? Mum? Arty?' Her voice was just a croak and she could barely see, it was so dark in the normally well-lit chamber.

'Is anybody there?' She shuddered as chilled air stroked her skin.

'Wake up, stupid.'

'Arty, is that you?' she whispered. The voice had been so faint she wondered if she'd imagined it.

A pain shot up Isla's leg causing her to cry out.

'I can move!' She investigated the weird tingles and stabs that slowly radiated through her body. It had been decades since she'd felt her own limbs.

The shriek of an alarm made Isla jump, and she giggled at the novelty of the movement. However, the continuing high pitched noise stopped her laughter. Isla realised she was alone, in the dark.

'Who's there?' Someone must have been paid to wake her. She twisted from side to side, trying to sit up but her muscles were so weak, Isla could only flail. She rested, panting with the effort of movement. The aches continued through her limbs but Isla began to buck again and after a few more rolls tumbled from her bed onto the floor. She gasped for air as her lungs filled with fluid.

'Mum? Arty?'

She closed her eyes. The only sound she could hear was the whir of the air conditioning. She coughed and swallowed mucus, finding it harder to breathe.

'I'm just going to wait here. I know my happy family is coming for me. I know they'll come, I know...'

This Picture Will Be Hidden

- Elizabeth Reed -

Lindsey and I are standing outside number 23 where, if there is a current tenant at home, they must wonder what's going on. Two women in long dark coats, we have already stopped a couple of cars parking there.

"I'm right across the road from number 23," I told him in the hospital when I thought he'd be out soon. He often talked about seeing what King Street was like after 'regeneration' and I expected to be able to show him. I was thrilled with my riverside apartment; delighted it was opposite the little terraced house, with its tiny, steep steps up to the front door, where he was born. I wanted to impress him with my post-separation bolthole in the old Albion Mill.

"Thass all rats down there," he replied.

It wasn't all happy coincidence to be living in his boyhood area. The walk from work to my new flat took me past St Etheldreda's church, where my mum married him in 1943, and anything which reminds me of her mostly makes me cry.

"They wanted it down there so 'is aunt and grannie could come," she told me when I asked why they'd got married in the groom's neighbourhood rather than the lovely church across the road from where she'd lived with her parents. King Street had been rough then: Flour Mill, Paper Mill, warehouses for the goods that had been unloaded and loaded onto river barges; shady dealings, fighting and prostitution. My mother shrugged, saying, "They jist took over."

"He used to gi' me sweets," Mum said when I asked not why they'd got married in King Street but why she'd married him at all. Another time she said it was to avoid being called up to war service as they didn't take married women. Gazing at the coal fire in the dark of an afternoon, she told me her mother should have warned her because, "she was born down there, she musta known what they were like."

My grandfather told her the night before the wedding, "You int gotta do this, gal Joycie." A few days before that there had been some sort of row and Arthur had squared up to my grandfather, maybe even hit him.

In the wedding photo Arthur is in his army uniform. He smiles without opening his mouth, because as Mum often said, "He din't have any bloody teeth in!" The army had removed his crooked and rotten teeth but had not yet replaced them with dentures. His full lips, jet black hair and eyebrows do have a certain appeal. The photo is of course black-and-white so his heavy lidded eyes, ringed with thick dark lashes, could be any colour however, just as I know Mum's beautiful dress was not white but ivory satin, I know those eyes were an intense blue.

The hearse pulls into the space we've kept clear. I wanted it to come to King Street first: where he'd started. I've asked for him to be taken through his city and the places he'd loved. There is no other family but me and I am glad of my friend's company as we get in the funeral car and follow the hearse - oh so slowly - up Rouen Road, past Normandie Towers and towards the city centre.

Arthur was always a city boy although his ways were country. As a child every Saturday he helped drive the cattle to market through Norwich for pennies. He learned the ways of farmers, cattle dealers and market business. Eventually he dressed like them, talked their talk, drank and laughed with them all day, then came home and treated us like we were no more than the animals he herded and prodded. Those horrible, smelly, shitty "slops" he would wear, like a brown grocer's coat, which my poor mother would have to boil up in the copper each week, and put through the wringer by hand, till she got a washing machine in the mid – 1970's.

Saturday night dinner was boiled sausages, potatoes and onions. A bowl of paleness, floating in that strange silvery juice it made. My least favourite meal of the week.

"Gid it down on ya," he'd say, slurping his food quickly, dribble hanging from his bottom lip, mopping up the juices with bread and HP sauce, "and if you can't gid it down on ya, gid it up ya."

"For chrissake Arthur!" Joyce'd say.

He'd point his fork at her and, with such a look, ask, "Do you want some an'all?" And we would scurry off to the front room and Bruce Forsyth as soon as we could.

Arthur had a lot of choice phrases, which he would repeat down the years. On smoking, which he hated me doing: "That wanta gie ya cancer." During my teens when I'd be dashing upstairs to get ready to go out: "Turn them bloody lights out. It's like Billy Smarts circus in here." And when I was ready and doused in perfume: "Phwagh, it smells like a whore's garret."

Years later I brought that up with Mum and she said, "Whore's garret? I thought he was saying 'Halls garage!'" We laughed. "I always wondered what it had to do with cars."

Castle Mall is to our left, which is where the cattle market used to be held and where, in the 1960's, the three of us would board a Red Car coach for Sunday afternoon 'mystery trips', ending up at a pub, sometimes with my mum playing the piano and leading a sing-song.

When we reach Tombland I see him in my mind's eye on a Remembrance Sunday. Standing at the side of the road, poppy proud, erect and smart in his Chester Barry overcoat and trilby which he'd take off and hold in front of his body in respect. He'd make that same gesture when hearses passed by in the street. As a teenager I'd be embarrassed by it, embarrassed by most things he did. Now I feel cruel and stupid, a renewal of regret for what never was.

"If you wanta git ahead, git a hat," he liked to say. He always wore one, whether it was a tweed cap, a trilby, or in a later years, a panama. He'd put it on top of his thick, snowy white hair, which would be in a short short-back and sides and Brylcreemed down. Brylcreem. That smell. He would have to bend a bit at the knees to see his head in the mirror as he slapped it on. Then he'd get me or Mum to make sure the back of his shirt collar was over his tie and lying flat. Off he'd go then for a lunch-time pint. This would be on a Sunday. The only day of the week Arthur did not work. He'd return cheery and mellow to eat his roast before retiring to his bedroom to sleep till 5 or 6. Often he'd wake grumpy and spoiling for a fight.

We near the church where I was christened, now Norwich Puppet Theatre.

After fifteen years of wedded disappointment my mother came home from the doctor, had a glass of milk – "'cos that was good for pregnant women" – and had to tell him she's having a baby, a baby that couldn't be his because they'd never consummated their marriage. ("He jist cou'n't do it," she told me with that same shrug of the shoulders when I asked the inevitable 'why?') He gave her a clout that day. But that wasn't the first time. The first time was when he took her to the Firs speedway, early in their marriage ("I dint like it, all the muck and noise, and 'e got raw."). He dragged her along the road then slapped her face and she was shamed because the girls from the shoe factory, where she worked, were watching.

Was any part of him glad to be having a child even though that child wasn't really his own? His name went on my birth certificate under 'Father'. On his own birth certificate that space had been left blank. They say his mother had a chap that ran away but there's a darker version: one of her brothers who'd lived in the house had fathered him.

"You're the best little gal I're got," he'd say when I was small and he was in a good mood.

"Well I'm the only little girl you've got!" I'd reply.

Heading up Barrack Street now, towards the brewery where he worked as a drayman for forty years. A lifetime of overalls featuring the brewer's logo. Even at home he wore his old bib-and-brace overalls, usually with a string vest underneath, showing milk-white flesh apart from ruddy forearms, face and neck. In winter he'd add an old shirt with a frayed collar. He always wore his 'slipshoes' which he would put on as soon as his work boots or best shoes were off. A man who loved cleaning and polishing his shoes, on Sunday mornings he'd spread newspaper out on the floor and get the tin of polishes, brushes and rags from the cupboard and care for those shoes or boots like he cared for nothing else.

Except there were the drayhorses, I suppose. He cared about them. His picture, very large, was in the paper once when the Evening News ran a story about him rescuing the horses from a fire in the brewery stables. I have that cutting. Along with working hard all his life and generally being the first at the bar with his money out, that made me proud. There are also pictures of the draymen taking the horses into the sea at Yarmouth one year, the only time I ever saw him in swimming trunks or indeed anywhere near the sea. When I was about five years old he lifted me up onto one of the horses and the height terrified me.

So we pass the site of the old Pockthorpe brewery and of the small cottage Arthur rented from the brewery, where I was born (and where he got a paraffin heater to heat my bedroom and Aunt Edna said, "You can't put a newborn baby near that smelly thing, you daft sod.") and finally, on to the semi-detached house he bought from the brewery in 1968.

It became Arthur's habit, once we moved here, to walk out every week-night to "get Joyce a bottle of Guinness." This was despite the fact that we lived next door to a pub and his job meant there was usually a crate of Guinness in the cupboard, and coca-cola for me. We never knew where he went for sure. We didn't care. We could watch TV without his running criticism and I could smoke. ("Blow it up the chimney," Mum would tell me.) At some point another television was acquired and so each of them had not only a separate bedroom but a living room too.

Approaching the front gate I can see four or five people outside on the pavement. Michael is among them and I am glad. In his hospital bed, the day before he died, Arthur had taken our hands and put them together on his heart. If he (mistakenly) believed we were reunited as husband and wife, we let him.

Mike and a couple get into the car with us, others drive behind as we follow the hearse down the street towards Silver Road; passing the front of the corner shop where Arthur dragged my first boyfriend from his moped, when I was 14 and out too late, threatening to punch him. The boy was older than me and tall. I was mortified but told him, "Don't you dare hit my dad!"

My dad.

The circumstances of his death continue to haunt me. The shock and the negligent treatment, not to mention the guilt, have made me angry and bitter. Again. Take a man off his stroke medicine and he is going to have a bloody stroke, isn't he? Fucking incompetents. Killers. Even if it's true I've wished him dead more than once during my life-time, he didn't deserve that. He only fractured his arm.

We move through the north of Norwich and head out on the A140 towards St Faiths. It is late April and the fields look new and fresh. For nine years I loved the drive this way, back to my marital home on the North Norfolk coast after taking my parents out on a jaunt or a weekly pub lunch, in a car I only learned to drive because they needed transport. I glance at Mike, certain that one thing he doesn't miss is dealing with the mood I might be in after three or four hours in their company.

I didn't know for sure Arthur wasn't my real father till I was in my twenties and one Sunday afternoon, visiting from London, I pushed my mum to tell me ("because it can't be him"). In between a heart-to-heart where I told her what Uncle Victor had done to me as a child for years ("Why ever din't you tell me?") and *Songs of Praise*, Mum explained my birth as the result of an encounter with a "rogue" on a girls' night out with my godmother.

"Whatever did Arthur say?" I asked her.

"He reckoned someone musta put suffan in my drink," she said.

He and I had always fought. Even if I hadn't been a cuckoo in the nest, we were so different with incompatible views of what a girl might do with her life, politics, friends, you name it. The problem was he had a frighteningly short fuse. Arthur was a big man and scary when angry, tongue lolling from the side of his mouth, terrible staring eyes, huge hands made into fists and not afraid to lash out. "Dorn't you 'it 'er round the head!" my mum would shout. And he would never win a war of words; a wilful little smartarse like me was bound to make him feel powerless. He resorted to hitting out because it was all he knew. Even the army had discharged him, recommending treatment, which he had never sought. ("Shellshock," my mother said.)

I'd been referred to as "that little bastard" or told "you're on'y a lodger 'ere" many a time without taking it literally till that day, after which, through my twenties and a good half of my thirties, I would never talk about Arthur without adding, "He's not my real father." I suppose Mum told him about our conversation, but Dad and I never acknowledged or mentioned it and nothing changed between us except that on odd occasions, when he kissed me goodbye or told me he loved me, he would whisper, "I'm your guardian."

Arthur's supreme moment came when I was nearly thirty years old and he was 65. On another visit home from London, I made a phone call to Ireland one evening to my boyfriend. Dad was angry, at the cost maybe, and the next day there was an argument. He came towards me with that wild look, his fists raised, and I was backing away but all of a sudden, instead of lunging to hit me, he reached out, put his arms around me and hugged me. He rose above it. I so admire and love him for that.

We turn into the crematorium grounds and I can see Jean, a friend of my parents, watching the hearse draw near. It was her who told me Dad was taking anti-depressants after Mum died. I hadn't been easy on him then. I wanted her, not him, and I'd thrown everything back in his face: his sarky comments, roughness and temper with her. But I did my duty. Not always kindly, but there we are. He told me once that Mum – when she was in a world of her own really, lurching between memory loss and bitter asides – had taunted him, saying that he wasn't "real family" and that I wouldn't bother with him after she'd gone. Poor man. I told him not to be silly. After she'd died his gratitude – his "There's on'y me and you left now, you're all I're got." – aroused such a mix of emotions in me that I'd speed home in the car, crying and dragging on cigarette after cigarette. Just before his death it became a little easier. I was forgiving him for living longer than Mum and he was indeed all I had left in the world. Now it's all over.

I give the eulogy.

'Arthur was a real Norfolk character.

In his time he enjoyed watching speedway, was interested in railways, trucks and vehicles, although he never drove, and farming matters. He liked military bands, Frank Sinatra, Glenn Miller and Morecambe and Wise. He wasn't a great one for hobbies or holidays. He liked the news and he went to bed early. He nearly always wore a hat. I remember him taking it off and bowing his head if a funeral passed in the street, or on Armistice Day at the remembrance services. He believed in smart clothes for going out and he liked quality. Most of all he liked to work. He took care of his health in later life and always insisted on good food. He was often seen at Waitrose or in the city, with his trolley, doing his shopping. He was fit.

In January he fell down indoors and broke his arm. After a promising start within the hospital system, things began to go wrong until he had a stroke. Possibly it is God's blessing that such an active man had health and strength for so long, without suffering a long illness or incapacity, but nobody expected this outcome from such a minor injury.

He was born in King Street in 1923. After serving in the war and a brief spell on the railways, Arthur worked as a drayman for Steward and Pattersons brewery. He loved that job – he was out and about, he kept fit, he loved the landladies and obviously the odd pint. It used to strike me that any street directions given by Dad always involved the pubs. He loved the horses and was so proud to display them in the ring at the Royal Norfolk show.

Some years ago he was pictured in the local paper with the story of how he had saved the horses from a fire at Pockthorpe brewery stables. I will never forget him taking me to school on the horse and cart, then later out on the lorry to Spalding with Terry Dales, RIP.

On a Saturday he went to his favourite place – the cattle market. He was a cattle drover man and boy, from the days they used to send the cattle from King Street and Rose Lane up to the old market, until Harford Bridge in his 70's when the industry went into crisis. He was so fond of his colleagues, as they were of him, taking him out on his 85th birthday last November.

Arthur and I were always grateful for the support and kindness shown by friends and neighbours, especially after his dear Joyce passed away nearly 2.5 years ago having shared 64 years of marriage.

Arthur was my dad. We spent a lot of our lives not understanding each other that well and I was often heard to moan about him, but we belonged to each other and we did the best we could. When he lay in the hospital at the end his constant refrain to me was "I love you ol' daarlin'" and "God bless you", interspersed with "How do I look?" which he always asked me when I visited at home, and, typically of Arthur, "Are you alright for money?"

I love you. God bless you Dad.'

We trudge outside after the service, which went well except for the undertaker playing 'In the Mood' instead of 'Moonlight Serenade' as the coffin went behind the curtain. I thank people for coming and that is when I see you.

A woman that I hadn't noticed inside the chapel comes up to me. She's pale and mousy-haired, dressed plainly. She starts to say that her granddad knew my father and while my brain begins to puzzle that out my attention is drawn to you, the young boy at her side. Your bright blue eyes, ringed generously with the darkest of lashes, look out at me from under a head of shiny jet-black hair. I stare back. I try to work out if you are her grandson or her son. You look at me with confidence; a sureness that comes from knowing something another person doesn't. I don't catch any names. None are offered.

I invite you and the woman to the wake at the pub. I am eager to question her.

You do not turn up.

Months after this, when I finally face going through Dad's belongings - the many biscuit tins full of bills and receipts for everything he ever purchased, death notices, telegrams arranging leave for a wedding – I will think of you again, on finding a black-and-white photograph of a boy in a jacket, shorts and knee socks. A dark haired boy. Too recent to be Arthur when he was young and too old to be you, this picture will be hidden at the very bottom of a tin, tucked inside a Prudential paying-in book with nothing written on the back to identify the boy, and, as I'll later tell Lindsey over a glass of red wine, I will not have a clue who he is either.

The Deal

- Wendy Gill -

And runner up in the Miss Newbury beauty competition is…
The alarm rings.
Blast. I'll never know.

My arm flops out of bed as I hit the button to restore silence. It's 6.00 am; the bedroom's a haze of grey. I promise myself that one day I'll get more sleep. Sliding my body snake-like to the edge of the bed, I lower myself gently onto the floor so as not to disturb Harry, then crawl into the en-suite. My weekday routine; usually my body clock wakes me moments before the alarm call at 7.30am. But today I've a plane to catch.

Out of the bedroom, I creep along the landing, passing the boys' rooms with the stealth of a prisoner making her escape. Downstairs. Our dachshund, Rosie, snug in her bed raises one eyelid, and casts a disparaging glance in my direction before returning to her slumbers. Half a cup of tea, bite of a cereal bar, pick up bag, briefcase, keys. Mission accomplished. I'm outside, they're all in bed asleep. *How much longer can I do this?*

In the car. I adjust the rear view mirror, and apply my weekday mask, whilst waiting for the suave, young South African lawyer who is accompanying me to a client meeting. A touch of lipstick. Check watch. Got to nail this contract: people's livelihoods depend upon it.

Where is he? It's freezing. Can't keep the car running, might wake the kids; and it's not eco- friendly. Shoulders hunched, cold hands clasped as if praying; a full body yawn envelops me. I shudder, helpless; mouth opening wide enough for my wisdom teeth to be extracted. Jaw cracks. Ouch. Holding my face, I look up the street for any sign of Andrew – or anyone. Check watch. He's late. Five more minutes. Maybe he's tried to contact me, check mobile, it's still on silent. Nothing. I'll call him… Adam, Akimi, Al Fresco, Alex, Alison, All Plumbing, Amy, Anna, Anthony… No Andrew. *Damn.* Check watch. Call boss.

'Hi, Stephen… yes, it's early. Contract negotiations in Jersey today with Andrew from legal. Don't suppose you have his mobile number.'

'I'll text it to you. What time's your flight?'

'7.55 from Stansted. I was supposed to be driving us both there, but…'

'… Get a cab. You won't have time to park now. We can't afford to lose this contract, Elaine.'

'We won't, Stephen. You know I always deliver.'

In the back of the cab, text message alert; Andrew's number from Stephen. Dialling. *You've reached the voicemail of…* I toss the phone aside and look up to see where we are. The driver talks into his rear view mirror.

'Going somewhere nice, luv?'

'Jersey. On business. And I'm running late.'

'Business. What d'you do then?'

'Healthcare.'

'You a nurse then?'

Now I know why I prefer to drive. Hey, lighten up; he's just trying to be friendly.

'No. I'm one of those dreaded accountant/administrator types. How long 'til we get to Stansted? My flight leaves in fifty minutes.'

'Why didn't you tell me? Accountant, eh?'

Reaching for my mobile, I bang my head as the driver does a James Bond turn, accelerating and swerving into action; only it's a Ford Mondeo not an Aston Martin DB5. Dialling Andrew's number.

You've reached the voicemail of... A horn blasts. Breaks screech. I grab the headrest of the seat in front to brace myself. The cab driver shakes his fist at the windscreen. 'Plonker!' A black Mercedes has pulled out in front of us. 'Think they own the bloody road, they do...'

South American salsa fills the car, getting louder: my mobile. I fumble to answer.

'Andrew?'

'Who's Andrew?'

'Oh it's you, Harry.'

'Good morning to you too, Darling.'

'Well it's not. And he's the lawyer, who's supposed to be accompanying me to Jersey, but he hasn't showed up. Everything alright? Can't talk for long. Thought that was him finally calling.'

'Well you might have to come back, anyway. Debs hasn't showed up either.'

'I can't do that. This meeting's far too important: I'm up before the Group Board next week. I'm sure she'll turn up, she knows I'm in Jersey today. You can cope can't you?'

'I woke up this morning contemplating our divorce.'

'What?'

'You heard. We're supposed to be moving house and all you can think about is work.'

'Without my job we wouldn't be able to think about moving. Are the boys even awake yet?'

'No. Thankfully.'

'Listen. I've got to go. I'll call Debs to make sure she's on her way. See you later.'

'Don't forget my league match tonight. The Club championship is riding on it. *Don't* be late.'

That's right, Harry, put your tennis first. Thumping my fists down beside me, I catch my hand on the seat belt buckle and look up to the heavens: the sight of the dirty cab ceiling brings me sharply back to earth. The driver looks up at his mirror again:

'How old are your kids, then? Mine...'

Salsa music. Saved by the phone.

'Andrew. Where are you?'

'In a cab. You might not believe this, but I don't use an alarm, 'cos normally the woman in the flat upstairs wakes me every morning with her stilettos…'

'Sorry?'

'…as she walks across the floor above. But today 'cos I had to get up before she did I set an alarm, but for some reason it didn't go off. '

'Right. Anyway, looks like I'll get there first. Meet me at the check-in desk.'

I look out of the window to check our whereabouts. *Absolute tosh. And he didn't apologise.* It's raining, a fine mist: waiting to frizz my hair. I watch it coagulate into a single drip on the window and follow its course. Bright lights and signs for the drop-off zone rouse me. Debs! I call her number.

'Debs. Hi. Is that Jack I can hear? You're at the house then – thank God. Did you forget that I'm off to Jersey today? Shouldn't be back much later than normal though. I'll call you later. Give the boys a hug from me.' *As if she could.*

The pristine ground hostess, in her calming baby-blue uniform and silk cravat, smiles as I arrive breathless at the check-in desk. I survey the Departures hall as she scans my documents. A tall, dark, suited guy is heading towards me. Andrew.

'Here's my colleague now. Will we still get the flight?'

'You'll have to hurry, they're about to close the Gate. You should just about make it.'

We hurry through Security to airside. Both carrying briefcases. They stop to search mine. Andrew looks smug as he collects his unsullied black leather case from the conveyor belt and strides ahead, whilst I stand, foot tapping as if about to launch into Riverdance, watching security pore over my contents; scrutinising a calculator as if they'd never seen one before. Now through. Running to the Gate. There's a lady in a hi-vis jacket with a walkie-talkie shaking her head. 'Gate's closed, I'm afraid.'

'But, they said we'd still get the flight.'

'Nothing I can do once the plane door is closed. Sorry.'

Briefly, I surrender; arms give up, bag and briefcase dropping to the floor. My face is molten with anger and frustration; I glare at Andrew and fire words through gritted teeth. 'I've *never* missed a flight in my entire life.'

He stares back, as if I've just told him I'm a vegan. The lady in the hi-vis jacket suggests we go back to the check-in desk for advice.

'There's only one flight a day to Jersey; we're on winter timetables now. I can get you on a flight out of Gatwick though,' says the blue clad ground hostess, still smiling, carefully avoiding our recent misfortune. 'There's one at twelve forty-five.' I check my watch. 'The train should get you there in time.' I nod in grudging acceptance. 'I'll print your boarding passes.' The printer clicks into action. Looking over my shoulder, space cadet, Andrew, is standing in the middle of the concourse, as if waiting to be beamed up by some alien authority. *That's okay, just leave it all to me, Andrew: just like Harry does.* The clicking ceases and I receive the boarding passes with as much grace as I can muster. My brow is fixed in a scowl, like an Olympic weightlifter braced to push up the final load. I'll have to contact the Client and grovel. Problems on the M25, I tell them. They are seriously unimpressed, but agree to see us later today. *That's what I need; to start negotiations on the back foot.*

The Stansted Express is an unremarkable journey, silent. At Liverpool Street we get the Circle line to Victoria. The Tube is busy. *Hope the boys are okay; should've asked Debs more about Jack. Little boy next-door-but-one has meningitis.* Checking my phone for messages from home, continuing to disregard Andrew: I become aware of passenger turnover. Glancing up, I notice the young businesswoman opposite has metamorphosed into a rather dishevelled fifty-something male. Still concerned about Jack, my eyes linger too long whilst absorbing this new hirsute image. His sunken eyes lock onto mine. He coughs at me.

'I'm dying you know,' he says and coughs again. Sounds rough. I lean back, aware that TB is making a comeback. He holds his stare, awaiting my reaction. *Why me, why today?* Words tumble out.

'We're *all* dying, just a case of when,' I say, turning to Andrew; now the better option.

'Oh, that's nice,' he rasps, finishing with a fanfare of coughs.

But nothing more is said, by anyone.

At Gatwick we line up in a small queue ready to board. *Great, the flight can't be that busy.* I check our seat numbers 5A and 5B, near the front. Then I see the plane; it's a small propeller job, no more than twelve rows of seats. Suppressing qualms, I call home; the boys are fine, everything's good on that front. I've barely spoken to Andrew, planning to go through our strategy for the meeting on the flight.

Seated and strapped, we've had the safety demonstration from the only visible member of staff on the plane. *Be lucky to get a cup of coffee on this flight.* Taxiing along the runway. In the air. Watching the Matchbox cars on the motorway. Stomach grumbling, trying to push hunger aside: hoping Andrew didn't hear.

'Did I tell you about my problem?' he says.

'What problem might that be?'

'Claustrophobia.'

His face is stoic. No amount of management training can help me fathom whether he is being serious or playing me; to keep control.

'Really?' I reply, endeavouring to use a tone of voice not to betray my uncertainty.

'Yeah. I once had a panic attack at thirty thousand feet.'

I'm still trying to read his face. Stress speaks on my behalf:

'If you do that today, Andrew, I will give you such a slap.'

He stares back at me. I exhale loudly, straighten my jacket and return to the view through the window. Seat belt signs extinguished, I reach for my papers to review the agenda and objectives of the meeting.

The Client Chief Exec greets me:

'You made it then.'

Please don't blush. Blood rushes to my face. Apologising, I introduce Andrew, then step behind him to recover. Corporate HQ dispatched him to deal with the nuances of Jersey Law. By the end of the meeting, my cheeks have reddened like a pair of stop lights as Andrew stumbled through the legislative issues. Another meeting is required to finalise and secure the Contract: it's a relief when we climb into the taxi for the short journey back to the airport.

Checked in: Flight Information reads *Wait in Lounge*. I saunter around the shops fondling soft toys and Jersey-shaped key rings, looking for a small gift for the boys. I'm at the Duty Free check-out when Andrew taps me on the shoulder.

'Fog,' he says, handing me a voucher to get a sandwich and a drink, then he walks off. I conclude my purchase and head straight to the flight information desk. Our flight is the last one back to Stansted and the incoming plane is apparently delayed with no ETA. After pleading... *there must be something you can do* etc., I slump down onto a seat, powerless, and call home.

'Debs. I'm really sorry, but there's been a delay. You know I like to get home to read Michael a bedtime story and put Jack to bed. How are they?'

'They're fine. But, I have my art class this evening.'

'Yes, of course. Is Harry in?' *Fat chance.*

'I haven't seen him since this morning.'

When I call Harry, there's no response; probably at the tennis club, with his phone on silent. Looking around for inspiration, I spot Andrew queuing at The Island Market cafeteria for his freebie snack. I'm famished so decide to join him.

'Well, this is fun,' I say, peeling back the white processed bread to examine the filling of my sandwich – only identifiable by its smell – before taking a huge bite into it.

Leaning across the table, Andrew looks straight at me, unblinking. 'Are you for real?' he says.

Who? Me? Can't swallow. *Are you for real?* I disappear inside myself and take a look; then splutter mayonnaise-coated tuna as I digest his question instead of my sandwich. Peering over the top of my glasses, I'm not sure what to do next. Then a smile teeters across his face, like a baby taking its first step. And I laugh. I don't know why I'm laughing. But I'm laughing, and he's laughing. And I realise that I haven't laughed like this for a very long time.

Grabbing my bag, I search for wet wipes; none left.

'Here, have this.' His voice is like a warm scarf on a wintry day. Taking my hand, he presses a neatly folded white linen handkerchief, embroidered with the letters *AS*, into my palm.

'Thank you,' I say, through quivering lips.

Then, the lights in The Island Market go out. It's only 8.30pm.

'That's rather early for the only eatery to close, don't you think?' I say, cleaned up, trying to regain composure.

A lady at the table behind rocks back in her chair: 'The airport closes at nine.'

'Are you sure?' I retort. *What about my boys?*

'Absolutely, I live here. I'm due on an international flight out of London first thing in the morning.'

My face starts to colour, but I continue to interrogate: 'What about flights that haven't taken off?'

'They'll be held over until tomorrow. You might want to book an hotel for the night.'

'I can't. I have to get home. I've got two small children.'

'You might be lucky; sometimes the airline negotiates with airport authorities to stay open late. But, I wouldn't give it much longer,' she adds, placing her hand on my arm.

Back at flight information. A short, bespectacled man is in front of me, demanding to know about the London-bound flight; his voice resounding through the airport lounge like a Tannoy system. Standing close, to hear any news from the ground hostess, who is quietly divulging information, I'm relieved to learn that discussions are underway to keep the airport open.

'Well, you'd better make sure that happens,' he finally says to her in a whisper, leaning so far across the counter that his feet lift off the floor.

'We're doing all we can, sir,' she replies, in a refrained, but authoritative manner.

Ready for takeoff: I turn to Andrew.

'Nothing's going to happen on this flight, right?'

'What d'you mean?'

'Claustrophobia?'

As we leave Jersey behind, Andrew explains that his claustrophobia started as a young child, following the mutilation of his parents on their farm in South Africa. And he apologises; confiding that he missed the morning flight because his girlfriend had thrown him out the night before. They'd had a mega row and he'd had to doss down with a mate; which was also why he'd not been able to swat up on Jersey Law.

Back home, around eleven, I've completed my second round of grovelling; to Debs, and promised her a pay rise. I've checked the boys; both sound asleep. Now in the kitchen, time-out; making a cup of tea. Thinking about my day, my life. Harry walks in.

'Got the kettle on?' he says, opening the fridge and burying his head into it. 'Anything to eat? I could eat a horse.'

Judging by his demeanour and the lateness of the hour, I'm certain he's triumphed at tennis. I address his rear end. 'Match went okay, then?'

Punching the air, he looks out from the fridge. Grinning in his shell suit. 'Yep. You're as good as looking at the new Club Champion. Stayed for a few drinks. You don't mind do you, El?'

I fall silent. He fills the void.

'Your day alright, was it?'

'Just another day at the office, really. Remind me, Harry. What was it you were contemplating this morning?'

He shrugs. I hold him in my sight.

'Oh, that. That was this morning.'

And wait.

'We're alright, El... aren't we?'

Placing his tea gently on the breakfast bar between us, I give him his answer in a question: 'Are you for real, Harry?'

The Stairway

- Nedra Westwater -

The stairway to the children's suite was boxed in, safe for us toddlers. The steps were of a light, varnished wood. On the risers, in glossy pastel colours, were painted these lines:

Little feet
that are weary
or full of pep
and zest
climb up
these stairs
for play and fun
for frolic
and for rest.

Each phrase was embellished with stylised flowers. My mother probably wrote the verse with its echoes of Longfellow, a poet she admired. My father did the painting. During the war he upgraded the attic of our house, which had been built for his growing family. We had moved there in 1939 while my mother was in hospital with my new baby brother, Georgie, born exactly two months before Germany invaded Poland.

I was allowed to play in the attic under adult supervision. To me it was a bomb site in England: at five I had a vivid, if overly romantic, imagination, stimulated by war-time radio broadcasts. I disliked dolls, with one exception – a long-limbed blond boy doll which I named after Jimmy in 'The White Cliffs of Dover' (as sung not by Vera Lynn but American alto Kate Smith, a much loved radio star). Jimmy had his own little bed in our attic bomb site in Ohio, where, when not working in the lab at Wright Field, my father floored and lined out two bedrooms: mine on the west side overlooking the front lawn, little Georgie's opposite with a view of the back garden and the play yard beyond.

In summer the stairs led to a stifling den which smelled of insulation board even after it was painted. The paint gave the air a chalky taste and made me sneeze. My father was obliged to install an extractor fan in the window of the walk-in cupboard at the head of the stairway so my brother and I wouldn't suffocate. In winter we shivered as the ducts for the hot-air central heating system didn't reach the attic. Eventually an auxiliary stove was introduced.

Often I was spooked by the long passageway that led from the staircase to our rooms and shared loo. It was full of shadows, deep pools where monsters lurked. One day I decided to explore the fan cupboard – strictly out of bounds – and in a stack of *Life* magazines came face to face with true horror, the living cadavers of Belsen concentration camp. Those stark black-and-white images would haunt my dreams for years.

On the way to my room, I passed between a daybed and another walk-in closet – larger, stuffier, windowless, reeking of mothballs. It was crammed with Sunday paintings by my father, yellowed issues of *Amazing Stories* which contained his science fiction writing and trunks of family treasures. In the largest trunk, nestled alongside my father's Naval Academy uniforms, was a pair of Chippewa moccasins made of doeskin and decorated with fringes and beads – a gift to my mother on their honeymoon in the North Woods. I never tried the moccasins on, just held them to my face, breathing in their wood-smoke aroma. By the door was a dressing-up box which my friend Ruthie and I plundered on summer days, trailing through our fence-free neighbourhood in dragging silks and satins, accepting compliments and cookies from Mrs Gardiner, Aunt Polly Caine, Mrs McCool.

For weeks I crept upstairs on tiptoe as little Georgie lay ill with jaundice, sweating his sheets yellow. His room was littered with boy clutter, including toy cars, a two-foot ocean liner and model railway stuff.

My room filled with books and, as I approached my teens, the accoutrements of a tomboy world: a wooden sword and shield I'd made myself, a bow and arrows, a brace of silver cap-pistols. Two collections my mother and her friends kept adding to, miniature dolls and miniature china dogs, took up unwarranted space. Neither interested me, although I was obliged to write a thank-you note for each gift. From the window of my aerie I saw fruits swell on the black-walnut tree outside, horses graze in the pasture across the road, farmhands tie corn stooks in the adjacent field. I thrilled to the drama of sunsets, snowfalls and the wild storms that hurled rain against the glass and whipped the limbs of the walnut tree into frenzied dance. The tree was the favourite perch of a mocking bird, which, to my joy, poured out its song on summer nights. When the moon rose full, Flackie, Aunt Polly's mutt, chose our front lawn to tell the world of his adventures, a serenade I did not appreciate. Despite Flackie's monthly vocalise, my room was my sanctuary, my very own space, inviolate.

With time, the stairs shrank in importance. Verse and flowers turned embarrassing when I went to university, but on holidays I still climbed the treads to my room. Then, at the end of my sophomore year, I lost my nonresident tuition waiver at the University of Wisconsin. It happened because I failed tennis. As this was a state university, undergraduates were required to attend physical education classes for two years, which I found tiresome. It was more fun to stop at the bottom of Bascom Hill and chat with buddies in the radio station, where I worked twenty hours a week as a student announcer, than to climb over the hill to the distant courts. I went to tennis three or four times, not enough to pass the course. This single black mark on an otherwise unblemished

record cost me dearly. My father, furious with the daughter who
had let him down at the university both he and his parents had
attended, refused to pay my tuition. As a result, I was obliged to
find a job in Dayton, where I spent a year working as a copywriter
in one of the city's two major department stores. I lived at home
and commuted, travelling the nine miles into town by bus.

I was twenty and still a virgin. The men I'd dated up to then
were from 'good families' and knew exactly how far they could
go. In fifties America, necking was a sweet art. While I'd collected
a couple of marriage proposals, I had yet to fall in love. During
this hiatus in my university education, far from the relatively safe
choice of student escorts, I became infatuated with an older friend
of my brother's, Dave, who built fibreglass boats and flew single-
engine crop dusters during the summer.

Dave was separated from his wife and two young daughters. He
was a cocky, muscular type with twinkling eyes and no polish.

It seems inconceivable now that I should have been smitten by
Dave. No doubt it was a question of hormones and pheromones,
plus the fact that here was a *real man*, like my mother's farmer
brothers who jeered at my education and proper speech. And
Dave was fun. He taught me to play poker and fire a six-shooter.
He took me along when test-driving his speedboats on the local
lakes, hitting waves head on so that I bounced off the thwart and
thumped back with squeals of excitement. One night we drove to
Englewood Dam a few miles from home, and there under a million-
zillion stars I experienced for the first time the world-altering sense
of oneness with another human being. On the backseat of Dave's
car, I lost my virginity.

I didn't get home until three o'clock in the morning. I inserted
my door key quietly, but as I slipped into the dark entry hall, my
parents sprang, hitting, slapping. They had stayed up for me,
feeding their anxieties with alcohol. The dream-spell of my first
affair dissipated with the violence of their attack. In a muddle of
fright, self-pity, anger, I struggled to the stairs. *Little feet that are
weary*...My mother and father followed, flogging me up *pep and
zest, play and fun, frolic and rest* until I twisted free and fled sobbing

to my room. Georgie must have heard everything, although I have no recollection of his being there. I guess he knew enough to stay behind his own closed door.

The next day I left home, under protest, never again to sleep in the bunk bed below the eaves. Who helped me I no longer remember, but somehow I found a room in a prim boarding house in Dayton. The furniture was faux Louis Quinze, white with fiddly gold trim. It made me feel like one of those silly dolls in the collection I'd abandoned. The relationship with Dave staggered on for a time, drained of passion. One night we didn't go anywhere, simply sat in his car in front of the boarding house. 'I'm going back to my wife and kids,' he said.

Ensuing events remain confused. I couldn't stop crying, nor could I keep anything in my stomach. Slender to start with, I dropped a dress size. My mother installed me in the guestroom and nursed me to health with toast and bland soups, and soon I was commuting to Dayton as before. Friends in the advertising department jollied me along, speeding my recovery from heartbreak. We even played a joke on Dave. At the senior copywriter's instigation, I rang him and said there'd been a disaster with the boat he'd recently sold.

'What happened?' He sounded alarmed.

'To be perfectly blunt, it's sunk,' I said. I hung up and my colleague and I collapsed in shrieks of laughter.

When I returned to university the following autumn, I took extra credits. These, combined with summer school, enabled me to get a degree in three semesters instead of four. At Christmas I slept in the guestroom. My parents climbed the steps now to my room, where they had installed their television set.

Dave did not go back to his wife. In fact he visited me once at university. Out of context, he seemed dull; I was impatient for him to be gone. But he'd decided I was what he wanted most in the world. He wrote me a love letter when he returned to Dayton. It was filled with the clichés of the lovelorn – not at all his style. My roommate and I giggled over the letter, to which I never replied. I was a woman of the world now.

In 1963, the last time I stayed in the family home, the stairway was carpeted, its poetry obscured. At some point, our parents had grown tired of the racket made by my brother pounding up and down the steps chased by Toddy and Trouble, their skittish black cocker spaniels. On that final visit, I shared the guestroom with my blond toddler, whom my husband, a Scot, had named James. Dave happened to drop in while I was there. He seemed sad, a person unrealised. But I was too happy with marriage and motherhood to concern myself with him.

My father died of cancer the following year. My mother put the house on the market after coming to see us in Rio, where she'd met and fallen in love with a British expat. Following her death in 1988, my husband and I visited George and his wife at their clapboard house in a town not far from Dayton. George drove us past the old place, home now to another family. It looked smaller than I remembered, far too small to contain all the vivid memories of childhood.

I've found a picture on Google Maps. The property is enclosed in mature trees, although the dear walnut tree has gone. The house itself looks unchanged. There's a basketball hoop by the front drive, which leads me to hope that other children – another two, even three generations of children – have climbed up those stairs for play and fun, for frolic and for rest.

Pendulum

- Bethany Settle –

Shock of brightest light and first breath and clamour, noise. The waves of fear and joy and relief that rolled over and through her tiny body: loud, love, the sudden sting of existence.

Yellow blooming in her closed eyes, all the colours above her when she opened them, the shapes that danced. She grabbed for a foot and did not realise that how it felt to be touched and to touch herself were the same thing.

She was running, she fell with force onto her front, and it was her first kind of dying. The crush and terror in her chest, and she thought of the goldfish, how it had hurt on the carpet. There was a hotness in her mouth and everything looked so far away, and there was screaming, and then she understood it was her. Mother didn't come.

Snail shells and leaves and crumbly earth in her little fingers. The neat joy of moving a thing from one place to another and changing the world. Tracing the edges of flints in the path, how one shone and another was dull, and another was a face that she often asked questions of. The answers rumbled inside her somewhere and this was satisfaction.

They wanted her to get in the hole under the roots of the fallen tree. Although it reeked of devastation down there, the chalk like bones, the sad roots that were no longer hidden, they smiled and coaxed, and seemed to want it so very much that she thought she must. A small hole for a small girl, her knees dug into her chest, tangling hair. She did not know what next, and waited. Eventually they threw stones at her and she couldn't run away, tried to make herself even smaller, instinctively covering head with hands, then the sharp scream in her knuckle, hot release. Shrill laughter receded. The birds were silent. Her hand swelled up, she ruined her dress with blood, and when she tried to tell Mother no words could get past her thick throat. Convinced that Mother would take her by the chin, look into her eyes and see everything. She wept. But instead she was punished. Anna cried herself hoarse under the blanket, the evening weight of summer light filling her bedroom. When she finally stopped she felt a different shape, could hardly see. Everything had changed.

Sticky sap with its own peculiar smell, and knowing all the places where it oozed the finest. The beautiful peeling brown and gray of the bark, how it was always under every bit of her. High and safe in her own private place. Stilling herself until hardly she nor the tree knew she was there, forgetting herself and everywhere, everyone else. The sacred hush of becoming part of something. A robin perched and song fell out of its tiny beak and she was the song too. Only after, when saying her goodbye she clung to the trunk and did not want to leave, when she was once more Anna, hiding from them, did she realise the robin had stood on her hand, the lightest life.

How the fall changed time, because it had lasted so long, like an hour, and yet how could that be? Four bones were broken, her leg in three places, and she saw the white of bone that should have stayed secret inside her. By the time she could walk to the stair window they had cut her cherry tree down and it lay dead in pieces, scattered, for burning and turning to ashes. How wrong.

How bitter, to be protected so badly. How little they knew, how little any of them knew except her.

Anna's book fell open in her hands as she thought her favourite thoughts. A different world she lived in, perhaps she had come from there and got stuck in this world by mistake. In the other world, everything was a kind friend to say hello to. Closing her eyes, she saw the table before her, and the grain said hello, and the knots and eyes said hello. The top and the legs and the corners all said, hello, dear Anna. Hello, said the carpet, and when she pressed her cheek to the rough green of it, it said, you are my friend Anna, I love you. Each thing she touched or turned her attention to was so friendly, and she was equally as friendly, and loved them all just as much in return. There were no people in this world, and that was best.

Before she could stop him, Albert had pinned her hands behind her and she was pressed up hard against the wall. There was no rare butterfly back here after all. Anna squirmed and struggled. She tried to turn her head away but he was too quick. He put his tongue through her closed lips - the cold wet strangeness of it, in her warm mouth where it didn't belong! And Anna thought, perhaps this is what happens next. This is what they do behind barns and sheds. When his weasel-quick hand went under her dress she screamed high and twisted away with a strength that surprised her. Furious and red she stood breathing at him with her hands on her hips, but he wouldn't look at her and ran away. After a moment she ran too.

Sky and green corn, and the ground below her. The blue slipped past, beetles crawled, mice chewed, Anna breathed and thought. Clouds bloomed in and out. Anna felt like a great ship sailing through the air, calm, afloat. Slow. The tiny noises she heard, the creatures that tickled and walked upon her, none of them cared about anything, and so neither did she.

Jacob drew a rude picture and wrote Anna underneath and moved it across the desk under his hand, tapping the paper with one finger. When no one was looking, she turned and smiled at him, and then very slowly she let all light out of her eyes and her smile fall away until he was facing a stone.

When Anna left home, Father was angry, a walrus, Mother white and hunched, and nibbling at her knuckles. There was love tight in her chest that she understood would never leave her, but it was squashed by the other things that lived in there too; dark spiky things that moved about in the night, stole her breath, made her head and throat hurt. Father's shouting and Mother's crying went from being loud in her ears to small, far away, until they were so small she could have taken them in her fist and thrown them to the ground like old dried weeds. Freedom blossomed in her then, quickly from a speck to a great flapping thing that made her run and spread her fingers to feel the air move through her hands. Anna realised she could finally be quite alone and nobody could claim her or make her do anything she didn't want to do. She belonged to herself.

With every movement, in and out, Anna grew bigger somehow, as if her inside self was inflating further than her outsides, as if she were a cloud growing out from her own body. Raymond was sweaty, and she clawed her fingers through the curly black hair on his chest and thought in a fleeting moment of the word brutal.

After all the noise of the train, to lie in the grass with Eloise, spent with giggling, and listen to the gentle rhythmic whoosh of the windmill's sails was a blessed relief. Anna thought how nice it was to be outside and to be quiet, but with a friend. The solitude of silent togetherness.

I think you are a stupid little wretch, the man in the bowler said coldly. How the mood shifted and spun, the turn of everything, dizzying, like a wheel. Anna didn't know what to say, and how quickly the old feelings of humiliation grew up, rooting her to the floor. Her cheeks hurt suddenly, and she knew a deep blush had flooded them.

Why do you wear those disgusting clothes? You are no woman.
You're a sow.

Helplessness and fear clawed her fingers but her hands remained
behind the counter, and her bad knee began a rolling throb. If she
could only ring the bell, Jeffrey would come out and rescue her. The
man's bulbous chin trembled, and then she saw with a shock how
badly he wanted to hit her. He watched her realise this, smirked
and put his hands in the pocket of his overcoat and walked out of
the shop. The sound of the bell's jangle remained in the air long
after he'd closed the door.

By the sun-dappled river, she scribbled on the backs of envelopes,
tapping out a meter with the pencil on her wrist. Across on the
other side, a very tall and erect man rode a bicycle while behind
him, three children on bicycles followed, variously wobbling,
crouching over the handlebars, overtaking. It made her think of a
swan with scrabbly cygnets. She was glad of the Pill.

The smoky cafe, darkness outside, the vicious ache of him being
just over there, how his beauty reached out to her every time she
glanced, even most peripherally. With a start, Anna realised she
was not hearing anything Eloise was saying – again! She could not
help herself. Her miserable heart banged in her chest, she imagined
it wasting in the mean prison of her skinny ribs. If he would see
her. If one day he loved her, her heart would swell, she would
roar like a lion. The depth of her feelings scared her, she had not
known this before and she did not know what to do with it or how
she might go on making her way through the world, this city, this
room while he existed and was actually over there, laughing and
so very, very beautiful. Eloise had known. Kind Eloise pulled her
close with a conciliatory arm round her shoulder, and Anna hung
her head for a few moments.

Anna was awake but he was asleep. He breathed, here on her
pillow, and she savoured it, loved each breath. All was new, orange
gold new like the earliest sunlight. In the night while they slept the

world had changed on her. She did not find the outline of herself as she looked on Nick, could not see where she might end. She wanted to run down a hill or dive into the sea, but she hugged his bed-warmth into her belly and delighted in the sweet ache between her legs.

The day was ending, the sky bright as spice. Outside, in the syrupy warm air, Anna said goodbye to the sun. He laughed, stroked her fingers. At an intricately carved wooden table, lit by tiny red candles, a silent smiling man in an apron served them steaks on a board. The meat was streaked red, brown, black on the outside. Fire broke out in her mouth, throat and nose, a searing, spreading burn that brought hot tears cascading almost instantly, and she choked and coughed and had to spit the mouthful out. After a minute of tender concern, his palm gentle on her back – when she was really recovering – Nick laughed so hard he cried too. The love in her for him reared up then inside, bit her hard, entirely.

First came the smell and warmth of him, then her body, her movement as she shuffled closer to his back, snuck an arm over. He held her hand, and breathing him in woke her further. Slowly propping herself up on an elbow, Anna peeked over at his sleep-softened face, the slight smile he often wore. She pressed her face right against his back, breathed through the cotton of his t-shirt. Getting up could wait.

Nick was missing from the mirror. Wherever Anna looked, there were all his things, that he had held and used without a thought, on the last morning, when he hadn't known it would be for the last time, when they hadn't known it was the last of everything. She looked and looked for him, in every room, in cupboards, in mirrors. First thing in the morning, those blessed and wretched few moments when she hurriedly turned over in case it wasn't really true. He was no longer there. She felt she was falling, very fast, that she could not cry out or even breathe. She had torn out hair, slapped herself leaving marks that took hours to fade, had thrown and broken things, split her knuckles bloody on doorframes. He was gone.

Anna, on the jetty, was level with the lake. The water spread out before her. I am on the edge, she thought, laughed out loud. She had felt drawn here, oddly, this place she never visited, but as soon as the idea chimed in her mind she found she was already on her way. To walk or look or throw herself in, she did not know. The cheese in the roll she'd bought was disappointingly mild. Watching the light on the water, she tried not to think, of emptiness, of sinking. Then there was a robin, not at all shy, hopping about next to her, on and off her bag. Joy jumped in her, and, when she realised he was only after the crumbs in the wrapper from her roll, she found she didn't mind. It was still a robin, right here, with her. She laid crumbs on the toes of her shoes, marvelled at how he ducked and bobbed and was so light she couldn't feel he was there. She forgot.

Anna stopped to rummage in her bag for mints, and by the time she saw what was going to happen, it was too late to stop it. The man had come from behind and to the side, his pace towards her as steady as her dawning understanding of what would happen next. Fear exploded in her so overwhelmingly she could only freeze. Although there was no need – she would have given it, she would have given it to get his flinten, closed face away from her – he wrenched her bag out of her hands so hard that pain flared in her wrist. Then he was gone – she couldn't watch him run but sank to the floor, groaning and nauseous, feeling as if it were still happening, as if he had his hands on her and was taking from her.

Out the window, it was all just green. Shades and shades of green, and the sky. The tall trees, bushes, the boundary hedge, the paddock where mist sometimes rose and hares had fought last week. She'd been looking out at different times of the day, getting a sense of where the light appeared, the path it followed. Maybe she'd paint this view. Claim it. Why not try painting? What else, what's next? Maybe eventually she'd stumble on a path forward, somewhere else to take herself.

Turning to go and stir the tagine again, Anna saw herself in the mirror by the cabin's front door. A face that life had drawn lines on. I love you, kid, she said, to her wistful face.

Anna! My goodness… we haven't seen you in such a long time, how are you getting on, you poor thing?

Once, she would have stammered in her haste to put Susan Beresford – well, anyone – at ease. But that Anna was already gone. The body she found herself in now was heavy, unrecognisably so, it seemed: bloated, yes, chemically ballooned, but inside she felt full with a black weight. It did not feel like cancer. It felt like anger, and it took up so much room inside her that she found it difficult to breathe sometimes, to talk to anyone apart from Jane. Jane made her laugh when she thought laughter was past. Jane had no qualms – this was a battle and anyone who didn't see things on her terms could fuck right off, and right now. What would Jane say if this was happening to her?

Oh Susan, the time I have left is too precious for this, but have a nice life.

Anna didn't look back. The familiar constriction in her belly and the tightening ache of her throat quickened her step. She thought she would get in and reach the kitchen sink at least, sluggishly jogging by then, but as she flicked the gate behind her the hot slew began to pour from her, it went all over the path, it felt so awful.

She felt hot, but the white of the cover soothed her hands. She turned them back and forth, submerged them in the puddle. Anna tried to turn her face to the white of the pillow too, for her cheeks, but found she could not. No matter – there was the white of the clouds, their intimate transparencies. A rabbit. A crocodile. Once she had seen clouds become a set of stairs. Now she could hear a motorbike, out in the car park, and Anna found she could imagine a red child on it, no, in a red coat, and the child was being carried while her father slowly rode the motorbike around in circles, gentle, round and round, so slowly, while the engine purred, hello Anna, I love you, I love you Anna, I love you.

My Dog Is Boss

– Judith Omasete –

1

A legend is born

One winter, while watching huge fluffy snowflakes, falling swiftly and adding layer upon layer, onto the existing white blanket. I see my dad braving the cold to sweep drifts aside, then sprinkle wheat on the lawn and put fat balls on the bare apple tree for the birds. No sooner has he walked back into the house than the birds busy themselves. Times are hard, gone are the autumn days of plenty when tree branches are heavily laden with berries and fruit.

A flock of assorted birds: blue tits, robins, blackbirds, doves and pigeons feed together in harmony until a Bad Bossy Blackbird we call BBB chases them away. BBB seems to think that all the food belongs to him. He eats the wheat and continues to peck any bird that tries to come near. Another blackbird lands to feed and BBB follows him. This gives all the other birds time to eat for a few minutes until BBB comes back to interrupt. Then, all the birds waiting on the tree and at the top of the fence fly away. Next I see our dog, Syke, walking towards the door. Then a gust of cold air comes in as my mum opens the door saying: "I know you are dying to get into the warmth but I have to get you dry first."

Syke walks in and hops onto the sofa next to me. My sister

charges from upstairs, goes behind the sofa and brings out a snowman blanket that she got from our granny last Christmas. She covers Syke while saying: "Oh! Good boy, you must be really cold." My sister believes she understands animals. She gets a hot water bottle and asks Mum to fill it. In a little while Syke is snug with the bottle and blanket, and my sister is reading a story to him. I continue watching the birds until my attention returns to 14 year-old Syke. I feel he is the most loved dog and stories of his earlier life come to my mind.

My dog Syke was born on 20th August 1995, in Kitale, a town in Western Kenya. He had two sisters Pinky and Elddy, and three brothers called Pucky, Elgon and Bob. Syke was the most active puppy and always the first to get to their mother Myph to feed and only left when his tummy looked like a fully pumped football. Myph was a shiny black pedigree Doberman who lived with Malasha, a brown little mongrel of a dog. Syke's dad was a German Shepherd and Ridge-Back Cross. This gave Syke his lovely black back, brown belly, long legs and friendly face.

After a few weeks the modern home my parents were living in, located in Milimani, a posh estate with huge houses and well-tended lawns, was now teaming with six puppies and two dogs but was also full of rats. It was fun to watch Myph and Malasha hunting down the rats; all one could hear was barking, stamping, whimpering and heavy breathing. This caused so much confusion for the puppies as Myph ran across the house from one end to the other, occasionally trampling on them. The rats became a big problem, chewing anything they could find in the house, but worst of all they brought millions of fleas in. This made my dad ask one of his friends, who had a big farm 15 minutes out of Kitale Town, if he could build some grass-thatched huts on the farm to live in. Soon there were three grass-thatched houses, an outside bathroom, a pit latrine and lots of open fields for exploring puppies to roam around.

2

———

Close encounters

Syke and his brothers and sisters grew happily together, but five puppies had to find new homes and only one would stay with Myph and Malasha. Even though Syke was the favourite, and had gotten his name because he did not stop running around chasing his brothers and sisters, birds, insects or anything that moved, it had not been decided that he'd be the one to stay.

Dad and Mum worked for an organisation that gave advice to farmers with small farms, so they could produce better harvests. They spent hours daily walking in beautiful valleys and hills visiting farmers on the slopes of Mt. Elgon. One evening they came home from work late. It was dark and as usual there were excited dogs running about when suddenly, there was a loud pup whimper. Dad stopped the car and Mum quickly jumped out with a torch. She found Syke with his leg under the Land Rover's wheel and quickly signalled Dad to reverse the Landy. Dad then got out the car and took Syke into the house, to have a good look at him. As tired and hungry as they were, they decided to take him to the vet who lived in Eldoret, a neighbouring town about 39 miles away.

The vet asked Dad and Mum to wait outside while he took Syke into his surgery. They sat quietly, each fearing the worst. The vet finally opened the door and said that Syke had broken a femur and part of his hip bone but, because he was young, he could recover with a cast. After the accident it was clear that Syke was the puppy to stay. It was very difficult to keep Syke calm and stop him from running about, but the plaster did help in locating him in the dark as all one could see was the white cast jumping up and down.

On Syke's first birthday, Dad and Mum decided to give the dogs a fun long walk for a treat. They went to Kapenguria, a town north of Kitale, a region that receives low rainfall and has seasonal rivers. Myph and Malasha sat calmly at the back of the Landy but Syke barked at people, cows, goats and wildlife until they got to their favorite river. It was sandy, wide with steep sides and could only be accessed by going over an old bridge to the other side where the local herdsmen brought their cows and goats to drink. The dogs were pleased with their outing, running about, playing chase and digging in the sand. Dad and Mum got some big green wild fruits from a tree on the beach. These fruits were round and hard just like those used to play bowls.

So they played bowls for a while, until one 'ball' broke and had to be replaced. Mum went back towards the bridge so she could climb over the steep sides to get another fruit. When she got to the top, to her surprise she could see that there was heavy rainfall above the hills on the horizon. This meant that the river would start over-flowing any minute from now. She ran back to Dad and the dogs, told them and they all hurried towards the steep bank. They ran as fast as they could and, just as they all climbed up, the brown forceful water came dashing under the bridge.

3
Sunny and sandy beaches

My dad got a job working in Somalia. He had to stay in Somalia for six weeks and then for one week in Nairobi, Kenya, where his organisation's main office was. Mum and the dogs remained in Kitale but it was not long before she also left to work and stay in Nairobi. Unfortunately dogs were not allowed to stay at her new apartment. Syke, Malasha and Myph were looked after by a kind man called Ben.

Dad moved to work in Sudan and Mum stayed in Nairobi. Then they got offered a job managing a guest house on the Kenyan coast. At that point Mum and Dad were not happy being away from each other and the now one remaining dog, Syke. So they said yes! Dad left his work in Sudan and mum gave up her work in Nairobi.

My parents travelled from Kitale to Mombasa with Syke on a seven seat Station Wagon and had to pay for the three back seats, all for him to sit across. As usual, Syke was excited and kept barking at any animals he saw, and funniest of all, he was drooling on other passengers' heads. It was a hectic journey until Syke fell asleep.

Mrs. Simpson's Guest House was a small beautiful holiday hideout about two hundred metres from the beach. It accommodated thirty at a squeeze and was mostly visited by people interested in colourful tropical fish, birds and other wildlife. Syke loved this paradise, as he was spoiled rotten by guests who fed him at the table and most of all he enjoyed the company of two Dachshunds, Bumble and Titchy. The three dogs got along well and had a daily routine: an early morning work along the beach, chasing and eating Ghost crabs, having a swim in the warm sea, begging at the breakfast table, going to sleep, before enjoying lunch and joining guests for an afternoon nap. The peace and quiet would be disturbed by the monkeys coming for a drink at the bird baths. Titchy and Bumble would come to life with annoying barks, making Syke join in the task of seeing the monkeys off to the trees by the beach. Then it was afternoon tea, time for more cake titbits, another long walk and finally dinner. One of these occasions the three dogs ran after the monkeys, but instead were met by a large dog, who attacked them. Syke ended up with a rip in his ear and it needed to be bandaged. He hated the dressing and would paw at it and making it bleed all over again. One day at afternoon tea, a low table was set in the garden with china as white as snow, tempting delights and waiting guests. All three well-behaved and hopeful dogs were lying around the table, but Syke managed to get the bandage off. As he shook his head, all the delicious cakes and china were beautifully decorated with red bloody dots. Dad and Mum had to quickly take the tea away and start preparing it again, luckily there was a spare cake made ready for the following day.

4

New arrivals

After two years of beach paradise, my parents decided to move to Nairobi. It was two months before I was born and they were worried about living at the coast because of malaria, a disease caused by mosquitoes.

Syke and my parents moved to house-sit a three-bedroom house with a large garden. It was just perfect for Syke to play happily in, except for a fierce ginger cat called Zingy. Everyone thought Zingy was a boy until she had kittens. When the kittens became old enough they'd wait for Syke to pass along the corridor, then growl and pounce on him with their claws. He did not like it at all and when the cats went outdoors he would chase them. He became the outdoor king and Zingy the indoor king. Oops! Sorry, queen.

On the day I was born, a family friend called Joe came to collect Zingy's two ginger kittens as a Christmas present for his children. Mum was in the bedroom getting ready to go to the hospital. Joe was surprised to find that my parents slept on a mattress on the floor and was very concerned that Syke could get jealous when I was brought back from the hospital and attack me.

The following day, back at home, Syke came into the bedroom, sniffed me and lay at the bottom of the mattress. When Mum needed to leave the room she said: "This is your new baby brother, you have to look after him." Dad found Syke lying next to me, giving me a cuddle and snoring away. Syke understood that I was his brother and he had to look after me. Whenever any guests came to see us, including Joe, Syke trailed behind them when they carried me. Just to make sure they did not take me away.

I enjoyed Syke's company and learned to crawl and walk by holding on to him. The best time was during meals when I gave him all the food I did not like. Three years later my sister was born and introduced to Syke, who had taken a liking to sleeping in my bedroom. He immediately moved to sleep with Mum, Dad and our new sister. I am not sure at this point, as to whether he was jealous or if he was protecting my sister. All I know is that when she was asleep he snored and when she cried he put his paws over his ears and if she carried on crying he came back to my bed where it was calm and quiet.

After a few months, my sister learned to crawl around the house by following Syke and soon she was holding onto his tail and he gave her support as she walked. She also played on Syke riding him like a horse while she clutched his ears, saying, "Horsey! Horsey!" along the corridor.

5

———

Syke the hero

One night when I was two months old, after keeping my parents up because I had caught a cold, we finally fell fast asleep but then Syke started barking in the living room. It was unusual for him to bark aimlessly, so Dad had to get up to check. He reluctantly walked to the corridor and managed to get Syke back into the bedroom. Skye slept for a little while, then started growling, first quietly then louder and rushed towards the living room, barking as loud as he could. There was a commotion coming from that direction, but my parents thought it was dog and cat wars. Syke finally calmed down and fell asleep.

The following morning, my parents were shocked to find that someone had broken into the house. The stereo was missing and one of the flower pots was on top of the computer. Thanks to Syke interrupting the thief, it could have been worse.

Before my sister was born, we moved to a bigger flat. It was attached to three other flats that shared an enormous garden. This was haven for Syke as all the families in the compound gave him treats and he had more children to play with.

One night Syke was barking very loudly. It woke us up and we heard our neighbour screaming. We looked through the window and after a little while we saw someone walking towards our house. It was one of the neighbours. He told us that the scarecrow we had made earlier in the day and left standing in the garden had scared his wife. It made her think a thief was in the garden.

A few months later, Syke barked many times during one night but we didn't think much of it, especially after the scarecrow incident. The following morning, one of the neighbours came to our flat after she'd been to the butchers and brought a big bone with her for Syke. She said it was a present, because he'd saved her life. She told us how she'd returned late the previous night in a taxi and on arriving at the gate had been accosted by three robbers. They'd commanded her to get out of the taxi and show them her flat. They'd told her to be as quiet as possible and promised they wouldn't hurt her, as all they wanted was money, radios, TVs and other electronic items. She'd been horrified. As she'd led them up the stairs to her flat, Syke had barked, causing people from two of the flats to switch on their lights. The thieves had been interrupted and were scared off.

Chewing his bone and not quite sure why he'd been given such a lovely present, Syke knew little about yet again saving the day.

6
—
The big move

One day Mum and Dad announced that we were going to leave Kenya to go to live in England. We packed all we could fit into our allowed luggage weight for the plane. But there was a problem. Syke was not allowed to travel with us. He had to remain in Kenya for four months, to get a passport and have medical tests to see if he was well enough to travel.

When Syke got to England he had to spend six months at the kennels. This made us unhappy but it is the law in England for animals from some countries to be put in quarantine for some time, to make sure they're not ill and won't spread diseases.

We visited Syke at his hotel every two weeks and I enjoyed the long drive from Eye in Suffolk to 'Quiet Acres Kennels' in Peterbrough. Syke got very excited when we visited. He got lots of cuddles and treats. But it was always sad to leave him. Our only consolation was, that he was looked after very well until it was time to come home.

Syke now loves to be king of the sofa and I'm relieved to hear him being called for dinner so I can take my place and get comfy. Just as I do though, cunning Syke taps on the door as a signal to go out. Unwillingly, I get up to open the door for him but our cheeky dog almost smiles at me as he leaps into my warmed post on his throne.

The Sitting

– Patricia Mullin –

I used to sit by the fire, below the family portrait. I liked to watch the little strips of fabric as they spun around the orange light bulbs, creating theatrical, heatless flames. Now, looking up at the painting, I can see it is as artificial as the fire. My brother, Stephen, who had been sorting through the books, asked what we should do with the portrait. Burn it, I replied. He made no protest. Then he asked me if I remembered going to the studio. I did.

I had picked out a green dress; it had a little fish blowing a bubble on the front. Mother's cotton frock was nipped in at the waist with a very wide skirt. It was a picture dress. The blocks of colour contained images of Spanish design; castanets, a flamenco dancer and a Toreador. Julie wore a dirndl skirt with an off the shoulder gypsy – style blouse, a choice that exaggerated every roll of puppy fat and pasty limb. There were six sittings at the artist's studio; we all went to the first, but after that it was just Mummy and me.

At that first sitting the artist, Lucas Mirren, spent a lot of time composing the family group and then taking photographs. I was ticked off for fidgeting by Stephen, who caught somewhere between boyhood and manhood, was going through an unpleasant bossy phase. My father, who was used to having his picture taken, seemed to know what to do, how to sit, where to look. My mother spent a long time re–arranging her skirt; finally, the artist stepped forward and helped adjust the wayward fabric. His hands were tanned, large and square, with a scattering of freckles, as if he spent a lot of time somewhere sunny. When I looked down at his shoes, they were covered with multi-coloured flecks of paint and his corduroy trousers had smudges of colour on them. I remembered the pungent smells; turpentine and linseed oil.

Subtle adjustments were made to the lighting and pose. Shoulders were gently manipulated, chins were held between his thumb and forefinger and tipped up or down.

Lucas Mirren plucked Mother's gloves from her lap and then he made a joke of not knowing where to put them down, everywhere being so dirty, covered in paint, canvases or brushes. He made great play of leaving the room with the gloves and then returning in a clownish manner. I remember him as a tall sandy-haired man, craggy, charming and urbane. I remember him as different.

His studio can't have been far from our own house, because my mother and I walked if it was fine and only took a bus if it were raining. Although, it was far enough for my legs to ache. The banisters were a rich mahogany and when we got to the third floor, the carpet and brass rods were replaced by thick red linoleum, with tough rubber strips bent over the edge of each step. Small dabs of paint, like a paper trail, showed the way to the studio door. I don't recall being let into the house; no one came to the door or greeted us. Perhaps the front door was left on the latch, or did my mother have a key? Once I heard music floating up from downstairs, it was turned off abruptly when a telephone rang. I slipped out of the studio and lent over the balustrade straining to hear the distant muffled voice, then a door closed. That was the autumn I started school.

When I saw the finished portrait I was confused and upset. Where were my little fish and Mummy's pictures on her skirt? I thought it was a dreadful mistake; I thought Daddy would be cross. In the finished painting we were all in muted shades, except for our father in his dark suit. At first I thought my parents were too polite to mention the missing textile patterns, they seemed so genuinely delighted with the painting. Years later, when I asked,

Daddy explained artistic license to me. Artistic license had also shrunk Julie to a slender and attractive form.

I was visiting Julie in Islington; she had agreed to look after my demanding toddler, Chloe. Julie was childless and a generous aunt. Seldom free to roam, I relished my freedom and spent the day in Covent Garden popping in and out of shops and watching street entertainers. I bought a frivolous skirt that matched my skittish mood. By three o'clock, I was hot and tired. I settled for an iced coffee at a pavement café. On the opposite side of the street, canvases where being carried into a gallery. The gallery owner was fussing and waving his arms. A young woman with spiky red hair was pasting the letters that formed the name of the artist on the window. I looked on as the letter L was unfurled, then the U. By the time the name Lucas was completed, I felt an odd foreboding. The young woman came outside to check the alignment and returned to complete the surname. The next letter was an M.

I watched the pair inside the gallery deliberating over the hanging of the pictures, then went over. The owner glanced at me and flicked his foppish hair back. Immaculately dressed, he rested somewhere between suave and camp. He glanced over at me, expressing mild disinterest, no doubt evaluating the size of my wallet and quickly dismissing me as a potential buyer. I thought I might be asked to leave; the exhibition was clearly not ready, so I asked if Lucas Mirren was still alive and was told he had died a year ago. The gallery owner unwrapped another painting, it was a reclining nude. It was my mother.

I stepped backwards; my shoulder caught the edge of the door. I took an urgent breath, recovered and continued my walk around the edge of the gallery. From the canvases my mother stared back at me, holding my gaze, blatant and cool, with an undeniable sexual frisson. A fleeting memory followed; the tender removal of her coat, Lucas burying his face in my mother's silk scarf. The gallery lights glared white and hot, I became lightheaded and weak. That they were lovers was clear to me. When did that start, before the family portrait or later? Was the portrait just a ruse, a way of spending time together? As I progressed around the gallery so too did the images of my mother. I stared at her aging flesh, the inky rope of her veins, the translucent soft tissue and historical tan marks; a relic of our family holidays in Brittany.

I wondered when she could have posed. I guessed it was during the school day when Daddy was abroad. Her nakedness was unsettling. Our mother was sensuous, elegant and self-contained. Our mother, who made Victoria sponge and fish paste sandwiches and met me from school every day. Our mother who asked about what I had been doing in Miss Eliot's class, and when I was old enough and polite enough to enquire about her day, would reply, nothing much, housework…baking. Sometimes she would sing or hum a tune, while I skipped home beside her. I always thought she was happy.

My scrutiny of the paintings aroused the curiosity of the gallery owner, who asked if I was an admirer of Lucas Mirren? I found myself telling him that Mirren had painted a group portrait of my family. I told him it was mawkish, he flinched at the word. He went on to explain that artists have to eat, he was trying to be charming, but underneath I sensed his contempt. He asked if I knew the model. I lied and said I did not. I knew he had detected this lie. He explained that Mirren had not presented a canvas of Rachel for years, that Mirren devotees wondered what had happened to her. I guessed that such speculation would include her death. But our mother wasn't dead; she was very much alive, about now she would be asking my father what he wanted for supper. Father had retired, that surely ended her career as model, muse and lover. The owner was talking at me, he mentioned the private view and he dropped the catalogue and an invitation into my bag. I kept looking at his mouth, the rapid movement of his tongue and the saliva connecting in viscous threads; the heat was overpowering… the lights… his words… my mother. I made for the door and fled.

I missed my stop; the bus had already reached the far end of Essex Road so I struggled past the standing passengers and walked back to Islington Green where I dropped onto a bench.

My parents had a model marriage, or so I believed. They had their disagreements and irritations, but amongst their peers their relationship was held up as an example. A marriage to aspire to, an aunt stated, as I prepared for my wedding day. My late, failed marriage made me feel that I had let the side down. It was growing dark and the homeless were beginning to select their benches for the night, I gathered up my bags.

Julie had cooked pasta and opened wine; I went to have a shower. When I returned to the living room Chloe had upturned the shopping bags, and found the toy giraffe I had bought for her. The skirt lay in a heap; the catalogue lay next to it. Julie swooped down and plucked it from the floor, she turned the pages. I tried lamely to pacify her. Reasoning with my sister was always impossible. Julie, drama queen and snitch, who ran to our parents and blurted out everything from illicit smoking, to dire exam results. I could always rely on Julie to expose my flaws and misdemeanours with relish and at the most inopportune moment. Ours was an uneasy alliance.

Returning from the gallery the following day she said that they were far worse than she could have imagined, citing the painstaking level of detail. She said that they made Lucien Freud look myopic. I laughed at that, replying that although initially shocked, on reflection, I thought that they were tender and refreshing; celebrating the form of an aging woman. But Julie called it a twilight age; she said the paintings were repugnant and disgusting. Then more thoughtfully she said; Daddy's face still lights up when she enters the room.

The Sunday papers carried reviews and a feature article with full colour photographs. Mirren was enjoying a revival. A week later my father's car left the road.

His injuries were slight, although he was never quite the same after the accident. Mother descended into a small interior space, she no longer sang or baked. Her memory failed her, a stroke heralded the end.

The air in the house was heavy and stale and all its little faults; broken window catches, dripping taps and leaky guttering, took on a significance previously disguised by activity and harmony. Sadness was present in every lifted corner of wallpaper and each inadequately wiped stain. Stephen threw the painting onto the pyre and together we watched as the flames lapped the edge of

Mother's skirt. The paint seared, peeled and lifted. A palette of vivid sparks flew off into the night sky, as if the Spanish pictures hidden in the under-painting celebrated Mother's vivacity and gave flight to her spirit.

Empire Girl

– Anni Domingo –

'They've made her look so beautiful,' cried twelve year old Zaina, her voice low, her eyes luminous. She touched her grandmother's face with the tip of her finger and reached out for my hand. Together we gazed at Rashida, my mother.

The dark oak coffin dominated the centre of the sitting room with assorted chairs lined up against the walls, an ocean of carpeted space between them and the coffin. The open casket, with its white satin interior looked like a large, new bassinet. In it lay my mother, shrunk to child-size, like a serene, sleeping babe.

Embalmed, wax-work smooth and wrinkle free; her blue-black, paper-thin skin stretched tightly over the sculptured, high cheekbones, her once plum-ripe lips now slit thin, sealing the sunken, denture-less mouth. The elegant suit was still, covering her delicate, skeletal frame; stiffened hands had been eased into pristine, white gloves and were poised as if ready to play with the treasured string of pearls around her neck.

I turned away and watched the rain dripping down window panes shedding tears for the indomitable lady who had viewed this foreign land through them. I could almost hear Mama saying, 'Typical, it would rain today.' Mama hated the English winter.

'Amina, this country is too cold,' she said only two days before she died, 'The damp goes to the very marrow of my bones.'

175

'The heating is on, Mama,' I said, handing her a thick fleece jacket. 'Why don't you put on another sweater?'

'I want some hot African sun, some sweet Freetown sun, not more clothes,' she said, waving the sweater away. 'It's one of the reasons Dayo and I left England and returned to Freetown, you know. That and the way they treated us all after Windrush.'

I laughed and put the sweater around her shoulders, anyway. Mama said this every winter since she returned to England, her 'Motherland'. She had reluctantly fled her home in war-torn Freetown, to come stay with me as a refugee, ten years ago. Mama stopped laughing about the cold or about anything eighteen months ago, after news from Freetown. My brother Buma, her youngest of four, her favourite child, had died; another victim of the country's continuing war.

'You know what I wish above anything, Amina? I wish I could go back home before I die so that I can be buried with Dayo and Buma. That's all I want now.' Her grief was tangible, wasting her. Arms became thin as mango twigs, bewildered eyes, her newly asthmatic lungs allowing just enough air to fulfil her aim; to reach eighty.

I stared at the wet, colourless garden. A remnant of the past summer, the steel frame of the pagoda put up for Mama's eightieth birthday party and now stripped of its bright canvas covering, looked naked, ghostlike. Mama's English and few remaining African diaspora friends talked in hushed, reverent tones, their funereal clothes dragging the dull, grey weather indoors. Only the wreaths by the coffin added colour to the sombre room, the flowers' heady scent masking the smell of damp wool.

It hurt that because of the war I could not fulfil Mama's last wish. I could not bury her next to Dada and Buma, in Freetown. Back there her funeral would have been a pageant, not this cold, wet, dull affair. When Dada died our house had been full to overflowing, loud, colourful and vibrant. Relatives and friends arrived soon after the first radio announcement ready to lament his passing.

Even as a child I could not understand the national past time of listening to the radio's daily obituary announcements. Mama and the Aunties waited every day, chairs drawn up close to the radio, to discover which Mr or Mrs So and So had died, to ascertain the antecedents, the intermingling relationships. They listened attentively, wanting, needing to know the brothers, sisters, grandchildren, the first and second cousins, the cousins twice, three times removed, the names of friends, acquaintances and even neighbours of the 'dear departed'. Their funeral outfits and matching hats were always at the ready.

I longed for the once familiar African rituals that I had grown impatient with over the years. I missed the way friends and relatives arrived with their envelopes of 'burial money' to help with the cost of the funeral. This had nothing to do with wealth; it had to do with sharing, supporting, looking after your own, grieving together, saying goodbye as a community. They came to pay their respects.

A strict dress code had to be observed so that all who came to the 'house of mourning' would immediately recognise the various degrees of intimacy. The darker the colour the closer you were to the 'departed'. Immediate family and close friends were in deepest black, while distant cousins, friends, and acquaintances wore black and white, dark grey, grey and white or light grey. Getting the gradation of mourning wrong was hugely presumptuous, claiming a relationship that did not exist. I remember disgracing myself by going to a second cousin's funeral in a pale grey trouser suit instead of black and white or dark grey as befitted our relationship.

'Trousers! Where do you think you're going dressed like that?' asked Mama, fully clad in black from head to foot.

'It's all I have here Mama. I've come on holiday remember? I've not brought a dress or anything darker for a funeral.'

Mama had not accepted my excuses though; she went off tutting and came back with her second best funeral hat and a black wrap.

'Put these on and don't shame me even more.'

I won't shame you today Mama. Even if I am in a trouser suit and not wearing a hat, I am in deepest black, I thought as I caught my reflection on the blank television screen.

'Oh God,' I said and dashed into the kitchen to grab a clean tea-towel.

John came over and put his arm around me. 'You ok darling?'

'Reflection,' I said, pulling away from him. 'I should have covered the TV, like I did the mirrors,'

'I'm sure your mother would understand.'

'The Aunties sitting in there wouldn't understand though,' I said.

Back in the lounge I threw the towel over the screen.

The hungry mourners, having come some distance, sat sipping hot tea from delicate cups and saucers and ate sandwiches meant for the after-burial reception. I, however, craved the taste of blackeyed-beans and fish stew, or maybe *foofoo* and okra sauce. I longed for newly-baked rice-bread, or *oleleh* wrapped and steamed in banana leaves. I needed the spiciness of pepper chicken and hot pepper soup to take away the taste of loss. The food provided sustenance for our bodies, while long, elaborate prayers, descanted hymns and mournful gospel songs, upheld our spirit, our souls. The flow of Johnny Walker whisky, Morgan Dark Rum and Star beer helped loud expressions of lamentations to flow throughout the night-long wake.

In Freetown, bereaved families were expected to spend time grieving not cooking or providing food for sympathisers who stayed day and night to 'keep company' with the living and the dead. For the first month after Dada died, houseboys or children of friends and relatives arrived daily with food in bowls wrapped in white cloths, balanced precariously on their heads. Out in the yard, however, firewood was chopped, meats cut, vegetables peeled, huge pots balanced on cooking stones. Children, dogs and hovering vultures were shooed away as neighbours and distant relatives I had not seen since the last funeral, cooked around the clock. All this in blazing sunshine, amongst the heady smells of flowers, red and white hibiscus, exotic birds of paradise, yellow-bells so bright they hurt the eyes and mangoes, banana, lemon, pineapple.

In that other world, that Freetown world of colour, song and dance, life's end was a celebration. Mama's old school band would have tuned up by now, ready to out- trumpet, out-march, out-sing the church band. Representatives of any society she had ever joined would be in their starched and ironed members' uniforms, hats perched at impossible angles, shiny shoes twinkling in the sun, all ready to march the two miles to the church and then another two miles to the graveyard. No cremation for us, Sierra Leoneans. We needed a grave to visit, a mound to pour libations over as we communed with the ancestors, a marble headstone to drape our grief on.

Dry-eyed, I moved amongst the groups of sympathisers. I listened to stories; memories shared; filling in missing pieces of the puzzle that was my mother. The three black-clad old ladies, squeezed onto the sofa like a row of watching crows, were my mother's closest remaining friends. They had started school together over seventy five years ago, eight of them had made the frightening journey to England, by convoy boat during the war, sent on government scholarships to study in the 'Mother Country'. Now there were only these three left.

'You look so like her,' said Aunty Idowu, peering at me.

'Rubbish,' said Aunty Modu firmly. 'Amina looks just like Dayo.'

I smiled but said nothing. This lifelong argument had always raged amongst my parents' friends. Personally, I thought I looked like my dad, broad forehead, small 'white man's nose' and thin lips, a throw back to our Spanish slave-trader ancestor. I did, however, have my mother's mannerisms, vocal cadence, and shared interests. Still, lovingly distant, we never did get past the prickly mother-daughter relationship. Although living in my home Mama still expected me to always remember that I was first and foremost an African daughter who always obeyed her parent and never, ever answered back.

'You're not going to greet your husband then?' Mama would say with a sniff, as soon as she heard John's key in the door.

'No Mama. He knows where I am. He'll find me.'

'An African woman should always welcome her husband at the door when he comes back from work; make him feel important at home no matter what has happened to him outside.'

'Mama, this is England.'

'No wonder there's so much divorce in this country. Go and show him he has a wife.'

Zaina enjoyed seeing me rebuked by her grandma, usually about my shortcomings as a mother or wife. She would collapse into laughter as I meekly went to give John a kiss at the door, a forty-five year old African daughter obeying her mother.

'She 'passed away' on what would have been Dayo's birthday,

didn't she?' Idowu said suddenly.

'Yes, January 22nd,' I answered, remembering that day. After just one day's illness, while the rest of the family watched TV downstairs, upstairs in her bedroom, Mama had some soup, drank half a cup of tea, curled up in her bed and quietly, suddenly, died.

'She never stopped missing her Dayo,' said Idowu, adjusting her too-black wig that had slipped sideways, giving her a drunken look. She stretched out legs that looked like felled tree trunks. Her swollen feet seemed ready to burst out of her black Sunday shoes. 'Well, she's reunited with husband and son now.'

'And Queen Victoria! Don't forget that,' cried Aunty Modu, grabbing my hand with surprising strength. Modu's lips trembled and her freckles, stood out even more than usual, darker brown paint speckling her warm honey coloured face, a lacy grief screen.

'Empire Girl,' announced Aunty Femi, her walnut shell face wrinkled and cracked like a dry river bed.

'Yes, Rashida was always our Empire Girl,' said Idowu, her peppermint breath, covering the smell of age seeping from her pores, tickled my cheek like the comforting caress of a tiny bird's wing.

'You know your dad's birthday was the same as the date of the Queen's death, don't you?' inquired Modu squeezing my fingers in her earnestness.

'Was it Aunty?' I winced, trying to extricate myself from her pincer grip, but Modu hung on, a clinging limpet, determined to have her say.

'Of course, that connection to the Queen was one of Dayo's great attractions for Rashida,' she continued. 'That and his dancing of course, they were famous for their 'Highlife' and 'Foxtrot'. During WWII, they were the only black couple in London doing exhibition dances at The Waldorf and Savoy Hotel tea dances. That's where you got it from of course, your acting and dancing.'

'I guess so,' I said, pulling my fingers away and massaging life back into them. 'I hated doing ballroom dancing on their TV programme when my friends were all doing The Twist.'

'Today is Buma's birthday, isn't it?' asked Aunty Femi, her eyes darting around the sitting room, searching for a glimpse of him.

Her mind was like a delicate spider's web, big empty spaces linked together by strings of memories. This was the third time she had asked the question. The other two looked at each other and shook their heads. I took the old woman's hand and it trembled in mine.

'That's right, Aunty,' I said slowly, patting the bony, clawed hand. 'Today would've been his fortieth.'

'Are we here for his party then?' She looked around with a slight frown and added, 'This hall is small for a party, isn't it?'

'This isn't a hall, Femi,' said Modu giving the other woman a slight poke in the side. 'It's Amina's lounge. See the photos on the wall?'

'Oh yes, there's Buma's photo,' Femi said, She stared at the wall of family photos before adding 'I remember, today is, Buma, my godson's birthday.'

'Instead of celebrating though we're cremating,' added Modu.

'Yes,' said Idowu. 'Fitting dates though, on 22nd, Dayo's birthday, Rashida slipped away; on 31st, Buma's birthday and she's laid to rest.'

The three crows nodded in unison, understanding synchronicity.

I had always known that dates were important to Mama; birthdays, anniversaries, the many 'occasions' were fragments, memory scrapbooks that mapped her life. She gathered these dates as aide-mémoires, an ever-growing string of date-pearls.

The significance of dates first became apparent to Mama on her sixth birthday. In the early twentieth century, the Empire, on which, (it was said), the sun never set, still commemorated the long dead Queen Victoria's birthday. 24th May was designated Empire Day. In celebration there were patriotic gatherings, church services and special ceremonies. In Sierra Leone, a British Colony, and as the only child in her school born on that day, Rashida was chosen to lead the celebration parade.

There were vague royal connections. Rashida was a descendant of Sarah Forbes Bonetta, Queen Victoria's favoured black godchild, and one of the Krio aristocracy. An orphan, she lived with her indulgent grandfather, Caleb Athanasius Gabbidon. He was a charismatic man, well over six feet tall with a voice as deep as the roots of the country's famous cotton tree. At the end of the 1800's he had left Freetown for the Congo jungle. No one knew exactly what happened there but he came back a rich man. Travelling to England between the wars, he returned with Austin cars to start the first taxi service in Sierra Leone, the first African to own his own car. He also came back with an English secretary who when she returned to England left behind her freckled-face, golden-brown daughter, Mary, Modu's mother.

On Empire Day, Rashida lined up with the other children, the flags and banners, the military and police bands, to march past the cheering crowds. Her starched uniform was cardboard stiff; her new black shoes, (with room for her feet to grow) were still too big, even with two pairs of gleaming white socks; her hair was plaited in scalp-wrenching corn rows, head hot, the straw hat prickly, stinging sweat that she dared not wipe away with her white gloves, dripped into her eyes.

Rashida, a natural performer, still smiled, despite being thirsty and tired after an hour's march in the blazing sun. Her arms swung in perfect time to the music, never missing a beat. The parade entered the stadium, to march past the podium, where the dignitaries sat in the shade, behind the new Governor - the King's representative. Resplendent in gleaming white uniform, emblazoned with medals, in the heat his face was as red as the plume nodding on his pith helmet. He took the salute before reading the Sovereign's speech to the nations. His wife, after patting the cheek of the little black 'Empire Day Girl' who had marched so beautifully, checked her white gloved hand - and Rashida Cecilia Harding acquired her first date-pearl for her memory necklace.

'Mum, the cars are here,' called Zaina.

'Where is Rashida? I haven't seen her since I arrived,' said Femi frowning.

'Rashida's over there Aunty,' I said, pointing at the coffin, trying to bring her back to reality. 'We're taking her to church now.'

'Good, I like hymns, don't you?' she said cheerfully. 'Is Rashida going to sing? She has a lovely voice you know, soprano.'

'No, Mama isn't singing today. Zaina, my daughter, is going to sing. Remember? It's Rashida's funeral.'

'Rashida's funeral?' Femi whispered, eyes welling up as she

absorbed the information. 'Is she dead then?' Her wrinkles channelled rivulets of tears down her face. I hugged her but I knew that her friend's death would register only for a moment before it once again slipped through her Alzheimer-sieved brain.

As I held the old woman in my arms I, at last, began to understand my mother, to understand her fear of lacunae, of losing fragments of herself into calendar-less black holes. Now I could comprehend her need for reference points; dates matching interlocking pictures on the mosaic puzzle box of her life. Understanding, I accepted her legacy; her string of date-pearl memories binding family and friends. Suddenly from the maelstrom of repressed emotions, a sob exploded; a lament for my mother, Rashida – Empire Girl.

Persephone

– Rowan Whiteside –

Persephone: a four syllable word, a name, a label, my daughter, my baby. That photo emblazoned across newspapers, a gap toothed school smile, her carefully arranged brown hair. She is the centre of a screaming headline. A million people know her face, her name, her habits, her hobbies, her likes and dislikes. But nobody knows where she is.

I walk past the door to her room, stare at the pastel coloured P blu-tacked to the door. I stop, and hold my breath, just in case, just in case, and then fling the door open. My eyes are closed as I imagine her perched cross-legged on the carpet, adrift on a raft of scattered toys and books. Then I prise my eyes apart and stare at the empty room and smell the stale mustiness of once present child.

She is a mystery. One minute there, and the next, gone, vanished into a swirl of autumn leaves and cobwebbed air. It's witchcraft, magic, voodoo. Someone's cast a spell and now she's not mine anymore. Perhaps she's playing Wendy to Peter Pan, cooking and cleaning and being mother to the boys. If she were in Neverland she would be safe.

And not being tortured or raped. Not tied down and hurt. And not buried in some unmarked grave, a tumble of bones and teeth. She would be with Peter, dodging Captain Hook and teasing the crocodile. Peter would look after her because her mother couldn't.

I failed. Without a daughter I am no longer a mother, and so

I am nothing. But I scream and I shout and I make my presence heard nonetheless. I'll rip the world apart until I find her; prise open mountain ranges and peer deep into lakes.

Wherever she is, I'll find her. I'll venture to the underworld, fight my way through the dead. I'll survive through the winter for those first signs of spring. I will carry on hoping, believing that she'll come back to me.

I leave the window open for her just like Mrs Darling. She waited night after night in the ice cold nursery, punishing herself for her negligence, because of course it was her fault. Not Mr Darling's, even though he told her to go out and leave them. No-one ever blames the father, not even the mother. No-one feels guilt like a mother.

It was my fault- I left her alone. I lost her. She's a lost child, but I've looked everywhere. She's not in the last place I saw her, or hiding under the bed. I walk round the house and look for her ghost, search in the shadows and clean out the dust. She's nowhere, slipped in-between the molecules when I was facing the other way. So I search through the pages of her favourite books, the old, and the new, to find the story that she lives in now. But she's not with Thomas, or having adventures with the Famous Five. She hasn't climbed through the back of the wardrobe, and she's not casting spells with Harry.

I don't know where she could be. I don't understand a world where she isn't here. When I was first pregnant I walked with my hands crossed across my stomach, protecting my baby from the outside world. I was so scared of hurting her, so worried about everything which could damage her. I'd flee from the first scent of smoke, cringe away from mobiles, and refuse caffeine and alcohol. I missed my kick-start cup of coffee, and my end-of-day glass of wine but my baby bean was worth it.

By the ninth month I waddled and I moaned. The novelty of being virtuous had worn off. I couldn't wait to be free of my burden, to be able to stand up straight and not support my bloated stomach constantly. I didn't realise that you carry your child for the rest of your life, and it only gets harder. Now the burden of parenthood has been stripped from me and I seek solace in spirits, burying myself beneath the comforting layers of alcohol.

Once she was born I adored her; my crumple-faced infant. I thought she would grow up to change the world. Everything she did fascinated me. She became even more absorbing as she grew. She learnt to crawl and walk and talk. Her first word was more, and I gave her more of everything. I spoilt her rotten, yet she was still a good child. I knew her best, knew to disbelieve the letters home from school and the critical comments from my mother. I knew that I was lucky, blessed even. My little girl was perfect and whole and clever and beautiful, and I was smug. Maybe I deserved it to happen, but she didn't.

I forgot to worry after she was born. I couldn't comprehend anyone or anything damaging this perfect little thing. I thought her impervious from harm and pain. Why would anyone hurt her? How could anything hurt her? Suddenly I believed in a world where people were good, and I forgot to be cynical. I was happy and stupid. I should have been more alert, for poisoned apples and uncovered wells. I should have been waiting for the worst to happen. I should have been prepared.

Sometimes I sit at the kitchen table and stare into the dark garden. Let my mind go blank and tick through the million different scenarios which crouch in the back of my brain, waiting to attack. In the best she is happy and safe, staying with some long forgotten friend or relative. Or she just wandered too far and was found by someone who hasn't got a TV or a radio and, unaware of her family, have adopted her and are caring for her. Maybe she was kidnapped by someone who wanted a child, and didn't understand that she already belonged to us. Those are the rare ones; the ones where she is ok and almost happy.

Then there are the others. Where she's tied down and cold and hungry, with bruises splattered across her body. Where there's an ever present video camera, and she cries almost constantly, eyes empty and soul broken. She might be locked in a cellar where there's a man in the corner, who's there all the time. Her body will be bony, the veins standing blue against her pale skin and knotted hair draped across her shoulders. Or, (and I can't decide if this is better or worse) she's hidden in a shallow grave, flesh rotting, with insects buried within her.

I wake with her scream in my ears. It's not the cry of a hungry baby, or the protest of an angry toddler. It's a wail of pain and terror, a siren which melts my blood. So I leap out of bed and race around the house, hopeful that this time I will find her, and soothe her pains, but I can't ever find the source of the noise. I hate to be asleep and unaware, but still I force myself to bed every night and sleep with the aid of tablets and alcohol and the occasional furtive joint. Otherwise I lie and think of nightmares.

It's been too long for her to be gone. The odds are against us. She is a statistic, another missing child; presumed dead. To the policemen she's an unsolvable case, bad publicity for the force. To the newsreader she's a school-photo; a good leading story. I can't blame them for not thinking of her as a little girl who's gone, or the family she left behind.

I never thought about other people's horror, because thinking about it makes it real, into a possibility. It means it could happen to you. So you pretend that whoever's hurt isn't a person because ignorance is bliss.

Except I don't get to choose innocence anymore. I wish I was still blind to evil. I wish I didn't dream of hell, and the people who belong there. I would give anything to be the person who got to ignore the leading horror story in the news, anything to be a spectator than to have to live in it.

I wasn't careful enough. I was too busy doing the things that had to be done to think about everything else. The petty flotsam of everyday life interferes with the things that actually matter. Now the mistake's been made and it's too late. I've truly fucked up. There's no fixing it and there's no going back. I've been shown the world and it's gory.

She could have been taken by someone we know (because that happens) or by a stranger. Did I tell her enough times about strangers? That she should not be fooled by offers of sweets or temptations of kittens. Did I warn her that there were nasty people in the world? Did the school say so too? Is there a white van out there somewhere with her DNA smeared upon it, and can they check them all just to be sure?

I imagine the person who's taken her and I know I could kill them. Eviscerate them with my bare hands. String them up and torture them. I imagine it's a man who's stolen my child (most of the comments on the *Daily Mail* yell "PAEDOPHILE, PAEDOPHILE!" and every other says that I should've been a better parent, that it would never happen to them because they know how to look after their children). I never read the *Daily Mail* before, but now I walk to the Newsagents to buy it at 7am every morning. I pore over their conspiracy theories in the hope of finding a lead, highlighting anything which might be a hint.

I've never eaten meat, I'm a pacifist, and I don't believe in violence. I didn't use to believe in killing anything. I used to argue against capital punishment, convinced that nobody deserves to be punished by death. Now I fantasise about murdering my daughter's kidnapper. I want revenge.

I read all the miracles, about children being found after having disappeared. Sometimes people send me clippings; push them through the door of my house, snatching their hand away before the letterbox snaps shut on their fingers. I see them walk away, quickly, as if the disease of a lost child can be caught.

Those lost children haven't been to Neverland or Narnia. Instead they've been living through horrors unimaginable. Or, worse, they suffer through horrors that someone has imagined for them. Those children were taken, not lost. Sometimes they reappear a year later, or ten, or twenty, alive but changed. Older and desperate, rescued, but somehow still left behind. So I will find her now, before too much damage is done.

Everybody else has given up. They look at me as if I'm mad. They pity me, not only for being careless enough to have lost my daughter, but because I am crazy enough to think she's still alive. I should've given up by now. I should realise that it's hopeless. But I refuse to give up on my daughter. I refuse to begin to forget her. She may have disappeared, but she still has to be somewhere.

I live only to wait for her to return. When I find her again I will make my decision. If she is dead, I shall follow her. If she's alive I will fix her. I will take the broken pieces of her and glue them back together with fairytales and endless love. I will make her forget what happened to her, I will make her good as new. As good as she was before I lost her.

She will be older, with new scars and bad memories. She might have developed hips and breasts, her hair might be longer and darker. She might not be the daughter I lost. She might not remember me or her father, or her cat, Mog. She might come into the house and not recognise her room. She may have forgotten the words to her favourite songs, or no longer know the stories in her books. She will have changed.

But she would be mine again.

Lion Bastard

– Deborah Arnander –

When I saw Lee's dad, I was surprised how young he was. I'd imagined him an old man, silent and suspicious in a cardigan. Clive had cropped hair and a very round head and, when he smiled, big teeth too gleeful for his face. He was wearing jogging trousers and a plain sweatshirt, and he was trim and springy-looking, like a PE teacher or an army man. He didn't get up when we came in and I stood halfway across the rug until he pointed at the couch and said, Well sit down, babe, and to Lee he said, Go on then, make us all a cup of tea.

I sat and pulled my skirt over my knees. Clive asked me where I lived, and when I told him he said Lee must be doing something right. A girl of about ten with long red hair in a plait looked round the door. As she made her way over to the other chair, she said hello to me, and blushed, then blushed a deeper pink. I caught a glint of braces in her mouth. She had the same teeth as her dad but she was pretty, plump and peachy, you could see her in a bonnet with a milk pail on her arm. When Lee came back in with the mugs, his dyed black hair made him stand out from them like he was wearing a disguise.

So are you working, then, babe? Clive asked, and I told him that I was – in a shop in the Covered Market but I'd be leaving for uni in September.

Don't let that boy sponge off you, Clive said. You tell him he wants to get himself a job, take you out. Somewhere nice, I mean, not that UB40 shithole where he spends his life.

Lee blew on his tea and smiled.

Clive asked more questions. He got up and turned his chair towards the couch so he could talk without cricking his neck. When he heard my family was from London, he started telling me about his days in the East End running pubs. He kept a sawn-off shotgun behind the bar for when things got rough. He also kept an Alsatian bitch called Sally.

She was a beautiful old girl, Clive said, but fuck me was she thick. Remember that time she ate a pair of tights?

Jenny looked at Lee and giggled.

She shat them, Clive said, getting up from his chair and drawing a line down from his backside to the floor, out for a week. Like strings of sausages. I swear.

When it was time for me to go, Clive said he didn't like to think of us, out on Lee's scooter, not on such a windy night, and if it was all right with my mother I could stay. Lee had a double mattress on the floor. A psychedelic bedspread covered it. He had pictures all over his walls, sellotaped, pinned, even banged in with nails. One of the panes in the window was missing and he'd covered it with a poster of the Jam. All night I heard it, blowing in and out. Clive's room was on the other side of the stairs. I could hear him too, snoring and sighing in his sleep.

Next morning, Clive had already left for work. Jenny was in the kitchen washing up. I walked her to the bus stop and then back, through the village to the bridge and into town.

As I walked I heard Clive's voice and all the stories he had told. Some were scary ones about their house and what had happened there. It was council but it was very old, and had been a field hospital in the Civil War. The toilet would sometimes flush when no one was upstairs. Clive reckoned you could smell cooking too – pork, the smell of burning human flesh. One time, he said, the African mask they had up in their lounge came off its nail – it floated for a full second in the air before it fell.

He told more stories about his London life. He said he used to be a runner for some gangsters called the Richardsons. They made blue movies – what we now call porn, only more tasteful and the girls were not so hard. They told him he could be in one but he was a married man – even though he was only 21 – and so he did the right thing and refused. That was the closest he got to mentioning Lee's mum.

Lee was in the window of the cafe opposite my work, long before half past five. When I came out he asked if we could go to mine – he said that last night had gone well but we should be careful not to push our luck.

We took the long straight road leading to my part of town, the houses getting bigger and the dark trees lining up on either side. We walked in silence. It hadn't occurred to me, before I met his dad, how quiet he really was. My mother liked people to look her in the eye. Lee didn't do that, not even with me.

But when we got to my house everyone was out. My younger brother was at football. There was no sign of my mum. I took Lee all the way upstairs to my room, which was in the attic at the top, and then went down again to make us both a drink. He was still there when Mum and Dad came in.

I could hear Dad shouting before they got through the door. My mother's face was grim as she marched in ahead. When they saw me in the kitchen they didn't say hello, or explain what my dad was doing there. My father grabbed my mother's arm and when she tore his hand off he grabbed hold of me and started yelling in my face, Did you know your mother is a bitch? I half-wanted to laugh, they were so intense, like they were acting – but then Lee was in the room. My dad let go of me; he took his glasses off and rubbed his eyes. Lee said, Come on! He pulled my coat down from the hook and we were out and running down the road. We slowed after a bit. Lee said, Don't let them get to you, you've got me now. I didn't feel I could explain it wasn't what he thought: my parents never rowed like that. Before my dad moved out they'd sat me and my brother down and told us it was no big thing, they still loved us and everything would turn out fine.

It was a long way back to Lee's. The village he lived in was on a kind of island between the river and the ring road. Going out, by day, it was a nice walk, all the different bits to it, first the fields and the railway and then the soft boards over the river and the walls and noise of town. By night, the concrete railway bridge was lit up like a gallows in a horror film. Shreds of plastic and knotted bags blew in the dirty trees. On the other side, the path into the village was dark, and there was a sound of chomping from the cows that gathered near us by the fence, and an occasional flash of white like an eyeball rolling, and the warm smell of their breath.

Clive was sitting in his armchair. He was wearing glasses and had one of those red notebooks in his hand. He smiled when we came in but soon he went to bed, because he was on early shifts and had to be out by 5. Lee and I watched telly with the sound turned down, and then we went upstairs.

Lee wanted to have sex. I was worried about Clive; Lee said, We'll be quiet and anyway he's asleep. But when we'd finished I heard him, in the room across the hall, let out a sigh, and I lay awake and wondered what it meant, was he annoyed with us, or disappointed, or lonely without his wife? Lee said she'd left him for another man, and gone to California. That was all I knew.

I ran home in my lunch hour to get some clothes and left my mum a note. I started to write Lee's number down but then I crossed it out, forwards and backwards making a black ink square. The breakfast things were on the draining board: just two bowls, which meant my dad had gone away.

That night at Lee's house I helped Jenny make tea. She was quiet but smiley. Afterwards she asked me if I could do her a French plait. I sat in the armchair and she sat on the floor and I brushed out her hair, so thick and silky, you could imagine the crunch scissors would make on it. Clive watched my hands go back and forth. Clive smoked roll-ups, Old Holborn, the same brand as Lee. Lee chucked his butts out the bedroom window or used the ashtray in the lounge, but Clive unpicked his when he'd finished smoking them and put the strands of clean tobacco in the pouch. He was doing this when he next spoke.

My ex-wife was the one to style her hair, he said. I never got the hang of it.

Jenny kept her head bent over so as not to disturb my work. I could feel her shoulders stiffening.

When you were little, she always did it different ways – you had a proper little bun for ballet, and every kind of topknot and bunches and plaits.

Jenny said nothing.

She wrote to me, Clive said, that all she wanted was to smell your hair. He snorted.

No fucking chance, he said. I wrote her back, just once. You come anywhere near them, and I'll leave you fucking dead.

I glanced at Lee, still sitting on the couch. His ankles were crossed, his fringe over his eyes.

Don't swear, Dad, said Jenny.

I'm sorry, babe, he said.

I flicked the loose ends over and caught them up together in the band.

Thanks darling, Clive said. My baby looks so beautiful.

He came over and kissed her on the head, and as he did I saw him breathing in the fruit and flesh smell of her hair.

That night was Friday and he stayed up with us and talked. He told us a story about an old man at work who was always boasting.

You've only got to mention boxing, for instance,' Clive said, 'and he'll say, Oh, I used to spar with Turpin, when I was a lad, down at the gym in Kilburn. If anyone's been ill, he's had it worse – TB, malaria, leprosy, he's had them all. He claimed the other day he'd been the one to give Robin Cousins his first skates. Well this week the circus is in town and John the shop steward starts going on into some tale about big cats. Oh yeah, pipes up this Bill, I used to be a lion-tamer once. A lying bastard more like, says John.

He wiped his eyes with the back of his hand. Then he brought in some cans of lager and we sat round and played gin rummy. I thought about my brother. He was on his own at home with my mum, who would have gone up early with a book. He was always trying to get me to play cards. About eleven Clive said that it was time for Jenny to go to bed. She groaned but did it at a frown from him.

He went into the kitchen for a bottle of Bells and three glasses. He poured us all a drink and let Lee have a roll-up from his pouch, because Lee's baccy had run out.

Clive lifted his glass.

Here's to you, Steph, he said, and whatever the future holds.

Lee shifted in his seat.

We do all right, don't we, son? Clive said, but I know you'll miss her when she goes.

Lee said nothing.

Might be leaving here yourself, if that band of yours takes off. Then Jenny'll find herself a boyfriend, and it'll be just me and the ghost.

You might meet someone, I said.

He looked at me sideways and I felt myself go red.

He laughed.

I've had enough of women, he said. Never trust another one again. No offence to you, you're just a baby still. But they like money and my ex-wife cleaned me out.

He picked up the little notebook.

Every penny that we spend, it has to go in here.

He threw it down.

She stole from her own son, he said.

She did not, said Lee.

He sent her the money, while he was still working, for her to buy her ticket home. She cashed the cheque all right, but then she never came.

Lee flicked his ash into his palm and rubbed it on his jeans. Clive watched him. He pulled a white paper from the pouch and started sprinkling tobacco down it in a line. His voice was softer when he spoke.

You remember that green coat your mother used to wear, and hated, said it was grannyish?

Lee nodded. His jaw was tight, his eyes set on his father's face.

I went through the pockets before I burned it, Clive said. The pocket lining was picked out. I can see her now, with her right hand in her pocket always fidgeting, she must have been picking away at it the whole time, like some kind of nervous tic.

He laughed sadly.

Silly cow, he said.

Where did you meet her? I asked.

Lee clicked his teeth.

She came to see me play, Clive said, when we were kids. Tommy Steele was her pin-up and she thought I was like him. And of course she was a looker – there are no photos of her here to show you, and she put on weight with Jenny, but she was always beautiful. We were happy for a long time, even though it wasn't easy, with not a pot to piss in and us starting out so young.

Lee ground his butt out in the ashtray. Whenever his dad glanced over at him he looked down.

I never laid a hand on her, Clive said, her or the kids. God knows I've got a temper on me but I never did.

So why do you think she left you? Lee said, and his voice was very cold.

Clive took no notice.

She was always looking for something, he said. I've thought about it since.

He lit his fag.

It started with the Cinderella watch.

What's that? I said.

It happened when she was a kid. See Julie's dad was American – she was a GI baby, there were a few of them then where we lived. Big base nearby, most of the English men away, leaving lots of girls with heads full of movie stars. One Yank and they're down, that's what they used to say.

Lee crossed his arms across his chest and watched his father blowing out the smoke.

Her mum got married after the war. Four more kids. Julie helped look after them. She knew she was different but it wasn't talked about. Then one birthday her mother gives her this Cinderella watch – she would be about 8 years old I think. It's the most amazing thing she's seen – nobody has one at her school, and she's really proud, going to take it in to show them all next day. In the morning, though, she gets up and it's gone. Just disappeared. She asks her mother, where's my watch, and her mother says, what are you talking about, there is no watch, and when Julie keeps on about it she gives her a slap and when she tries again she gives her such a look as if to say, your life will not be worth living my girl. So ever afterwards she's puzzled by it, and sad, and nothing's ever good enough. Of course when she's older she guesses that it must have been sent over by her dad, and then her mother thought better of letting her have it, and took it away.

That night in bed Lee held me tightly.

Promise me, he said, for fuck's sake, that we'll never be like them.

We won't, I said, there's no way that we will.

When he'd gone to sleep I thought about his mum. She'd be waking up now, on the other side of the world, or drinking orange juice to the sound of breakers crashing on the shore. I pictured a white house on the beach, with all the shutters open and the sweet breeze blowing in. Wistfully she runs her finger over a picture on the counter there – the breakfast bar, with barstools on chrome legs - that she keeps in a driftwood frame: Lee aged about 8, sitting with Jenny as a baby, smiling and winking in the sun. She sighs and warms her hands – now she's drinking coffee – and stares out at the sea. Her face is changing: she was mumsy to start with, in a sort of Diane Keaton way. She's younger, blonder, wearing a linen shirt. A door opens behind her with no sound. Its shadow spills across the floor of the white room.

Appetition

– Bridget Read –

It was June, the day after Paul's twenty-first birthday. It had been a hot, humid Friday, the time of year in New York when the city's buildings and pavement seem to roast its inhabitants slowly, agonizingly; eight million people spinning on a giant rotisserie. Paul and I met after work at the 86th Street stop on the No. 6 train, tired and smelling like the subway, with a plan for dinner.

My suggestion was soft-shell crabs, a summer food in my family. I had told Paul about Saturday mornings spent at the marina in Southwest Washington D.C., picking out live, slimy, silver and pink soft-shells that had been brought in fresh from the Chesapeake Bay. My mother would spread them out over our kitchen counter, where they crawled languorously, and she would quickly and efficiently kill them: a knife right between the eyes, twisted up and out. Then, the cleaning, the skirt flap and gills scooped out and discarded. Finally, the dry-wet-dry in which the crab's soft, limp body is dredged in flour, then buttermilk, then back in the flour, before it is laid gently into a sizzling pan of oil. The finished crabs are crispy, and succulent, their thin shells breaking as you bite into the sweet, delicate meat beneath.

Paul wanted *cacio e pepe* – 'cheese and pepper' in Italian, a pasta dish named for its two primary ingredients. It was one of his favorites, and he assured me I would love it too. He liked the combination of the smooth, mild cheese and the spicy cracked black pepper, itching at the back of his throat. Recently, we had been walking on Second Avenue when we saw a restaurant named Cacio e Pepe, and Paul had said, 'Let's have that.' For dessert, I bought a banana cream pie from a Ukrainian bakery on East 9th Street.

The dinner was an attempt to assuage tensions between Paul and me as much as it was to celebrate his birthday. It had been a strained couple of weeks, both of us living in the same city for the first time. A few days before, I had dragged him home with me to the East Village, to help install an air conditioner in the window of my tiny, fourth floor walk-up apartment. It was at the other end of the city from where he lived. Sweating through his button down shirt, black hair sticking to his face, he grumbled through the whole project. I sniped back, and complained when he wouldn't lie down with me and enjoy the cold air after we – after he – had finally finished.

But we worked well together in his kitchen. Paul would perch at the breakfast counter at one end of the narrow space while I knocked my way between appliances, running from the fridge to the stove and standing by the open window when I got too hot. Paul always helped with the preparation – the washing, chopping, slicing, and grating – but he left the actual cooking up to me. Then he would sit and talk to me over the whirring fan above the stovetop, following my movements with his one brown eye and one green.

This is what I remember: A mad dash to Dorian's, a fish market on York Avenue, when the stores on Third and Lexington were out of soft-shells. Our shared relief when the woman behind the counter had enough for us. Walking, slowly and out of breath, back toward home for the rest of our ingredients. At Paul's apartment, vacated by his parents for the weekend, flour everywhere, caking the emerald green counters in the kitchen and the floor, clouds of it visible under the overhead lights. My frantic mixing of spaghetti in the big pasta pot, fingers tiring from gripping the spoon too tightly. I think I remember laughter – Paul's or mine, I'm not sure.

Was it at the mess? At setting off the smoke detector? It happened nearly every time we used the stove.

Eventually, we ate. I try to place myself in this part of the night, though individual moments are mostly gone. I can call up Paul's face looking at me from across the table, insert the components of this meal into familiar choreography. His relaxed shoulders, a glass of something, probably milk, or a bottle of water, to his right. Meticulous, slow cutting of the crab legs from the body. The fork comes up to his mouth. He chews carefully, with consideration. The fork returns, and twirls a long, pale yellow strand of pasta, gathering sauce from the plate. Paul isn't greedy when he eats, like me. I eat too fast. I take pleasure in the cooking, but I don't give myself time to taste everything. Paul doesn't inhale his food like it's going to be taken from him; he eats with ease, enjoying each bite. He scrapes the last bits of crab and pasta onto the side of his fork, collecting leftover morsels of fried shell and cheese. He does this at restaurants, too, leaving his plate as clean as if it arrived at the table that way, empty and glistening. At the end, leaning back, he exhales deeply. A smile if it was good. It was satisfying for me just to watch him eat, ardently and indulgently. Sometimes I wonder if I ate my own food too fast just to have more time to see him finish.

When Paul died, I had no appetite. I'm an emotional eater – food has *always* healed me, and I can always, always eat. During the worst parts of his cancer, I snuck into the kitchen in the middle of the night and ate chocolate chip cookies, sitting on the floor in the dark. The fact that I couldn't eat was the thing that really made me feel like the world had become a different one after he'd died. Not taking part in the funeral arrangements, or listening to our friends cry, or being in his empty room. Paul didn't feel dead – my brain wouldn't allow it – but I felt like a ghost. The food I put in my mouth, under gentle orders from my parents and my sister, felt like it floated right out of me. I said to them, 'Remember in *Casper*, when the uncles sit around the table and eat? And the food just falls down, right onto the floor?'

After our dinner with the *cacio e pepe* and the crab, I told Paul that I had thought about recording myself singing his favorite songs for him as a birthday present. 'I would have loved that!' he claimed, even though I knew it embarrassed him when I sang anywhere near him, like I did in the car and in the shower. He was being nice, because of the dinner and his birthday, and he teased me into singing 'The Way You Look Tonight,' as we lay in his bed, too full for dessert. I finished the first verse alone, then Paul joined me, tuneless and croaking, and we laughed. I was lying on his left shoulder with my head tucked under his chin, so I couldn't see his face, but we both felt the moment change, our voices, the only sounds in the room. The tune of 'The Way You Look Tonight' is bouncy, and, in the Frank Sinatra recording – Paul loved Frank Sinatra – the horns and drums of the big band keep jazzy, cheerful time but the lyrics of the song anticipate loneliness.

Writing about a dead person is like trying to pin down shafts of light. You search through memories, glimpse parts of the lost person in sweeping or minute increments of time. The images can run slowly, as if (locked) in a still life – his legs in blue pajamas, Paul seated in his desk chair, illuminated by the fuzzy light of the television – or whole years bleed together into colors and shapes. I've felt this way since the instant that Paul died, like I'm trying to find my way back into a world that is spinning further out and away from me with every second. Or I'm the one who's falling – dropped, as if I'm on one of those rides at amusement parks where they strap you in and let you go. Paul died next to me and I instantly began cataloguing thousands of memories, smells, sounds, words and touches. But every time I held onto one thing, dozens of others slipped by. My sister says that I asked her strange, unnerving questions that night: 'Did any of it even happen? Was he even ever here? Am I here?'

I've searched in different places for things that might help me feel closer to Paul. I take walks along 82nd Street from his apartment to the Metropolitan Museum of Art, a favourite route he showed me during one of my first visits to New York. We held onto each other and slipped in the snow until we reached the big, broad steps, where we kissed for as long as we could stand the cold. It's all wrong when I go there now – the crowds are too loud, the smells from the pretzel and hot dog vendors are too strong, the building's stone facade in the sunshine is too grey. If I walked in a snowfall, at night, with the museum quiet and lit up in warm, yellow light as it was when Paul first brought me; I suspect it would feel even more artificial, a hollow shell of a moment.

I used to hang onto Paul's smell until one day it stopped being his. I wore his sweaters and his T-shirts, trying to cover myself in those parts of his scent that brought a bit of him – just a shadow – back to me: deep, earthy wood, from the panelling that lined the walls of the closet; a suggestion of lavender, left by the detergent his family used to do their laundry. But those are only the things I could name that made Paul smell like Paul, and eventually, with washes and dry-cleans and times I stood next to people smoking, those unknowable, essential smells I couldn't identify were lost. A few months after his death, I recognized the packaging of Paul's particular brand of deodorant in a drugstore, and immediately tore a stick out of its casing and all but stuck it up my nose. A clerk found me in the aisle and said, 'You know no one else can buy that now, right?' For an instant I felt the vengeful urge to tell him I was inhaling the scent of my dead boyfriend. I didn't. I wanted to shield him from the dark, hulking cloud of emotion. After all, for him, it was just an antiperspirant. When I got home with it, I spent time putting the deodorant on myself, slowly dragging the cold, clear gel over my palms, my wrists, up the undersides of my forearms, and in the hollows above each collarbone. I finished, and breathed in deeply. It didn't smell like Paul, so I threw it away.

The fact that I couldn't eat in the days after Paul died made me think constantly of food. When people gathered at his family's apartment after the funeral, I walked around the rooms with a red tin full of tiny lemon butter cookies, hysterically offering them to the people around me like an overzealous grocery store employee. 'You have to try one of these, Paul *loved* them,' I insisted to his rabbi, his paediatrician, his SAT tutor. 'His mother's friend from Texas makes them. One weekend we must have eaten a whole tin, that's like, fifteen a day, each.' But I couldn't eat them myself. I felt stuck between worlds looking down at the yellow, sugar-dusted squares. I knew the cookies were in the tin in my hands in the present, at that moment, but they also belonged to a different time and place, where Paul was and where I wanted to be. Each one contained innumerable lost pleasures: indulging Paul's irrepressible sweet tooth, his body healthy and whole; watching him appreciate food like an elaborate gift, a product of time and effort and love, the experience sensual and utterly alive.

I eat now to feel close to Paul again – or, more precisely, to feel closer to that part of myself that was close to Paul, since both are gone. I'll have a knish and its mild, smooth potato insides will bring me to the first time I tried Paul's favorite Jewish foods. Sitting in his parents' kitchen, he and his uncle and stepfather laughing at the face I make when Paul tells me to take a bite of his sandwich: beef tongue with mustard on rye. I'll sit at a sushi bar – Paul loved to eat sushi, even when he was little. His mother says he liked it because he knew it wasn't typical kid food, far too adventurous and expensive. I'll watch the sushi chef slice deep red *toro* tuna and pink salmon, pale *hamachi* so thin you can see right through it, and think that Paul must have liked the intricacy, appreciated the expertise at work in each little marriage of rice and fish glistening with soy sauce under the lights above the counter.

But these memories don't flood in suddenly, rushing and overtaking me only to leave just as quickly. When I eat, thoughts of Paul fill me up slowly and quietly, and linger long after the meal itself is finished.

Tonight I make *cacio e pepe*. I plunge stiff threads of spaghetti into boiling water, pushing them further into the pot until they soften and swirl together at the bottom. I crack black pepper. I add water from the boiling pasta to melted butter, and stir in cheese that softens into sauce as I drag a spoon around the grey edges of the saucepan. When the spaghetti is cooked *al dente*, and the sauce is finished and the pepper is mixed, I swirl a few creamy strands around my fork. I let a drip collect at the bottom and watch it fall, a tiny splash of yellow against white plate beneath. I take a bite, and swallow. Pepper itches at the back of my throat.

Contributors

Deborah Arnander was born in Northumberland and spent her childhood in Thailand. She has worked as an academic, translator and speech-writer. She won an Escalator New Writing Award in 2009 from the Writers' Centre Norwich, and is currently working on her first novel, about a GI baby, set in wartime Norfolk and 90s California.

Sarah Baxter was born in Colchester and is the oldest of three daughters. She gained a First in Chemistry at Warwick University and a research career beckoned, before becoming impossible, when she realised she was allergic to solvents. After a spell in the Perthshire Highlands, Sarah returned to her birthplace where she discovered writing through adult education classes. In 2013, Sarah came third in the flash fiction category of The Bridport Prize. Sarah is currently working on her first novel.

Lynne Bryan is the author of a short story collection *Envy At The Cheese Handout* (published by Faber & Faber), and the novels *Gorgeous and Like Rabbits* (Sceptre). She is co-organiser of Words And Women.

Susan Dean has been filling notebooks with her observations on life since the age of eight. She currently combines working full-time running a small music publishing company with doing a part-time MA in creative writing at the Anglia Ruskin University. She lives in a Breckland town on the Suffolk/Norfolk border.

Anni Domingo is an actress living out in the Fens. She has worked extensively in the UK and abroad in theatre, radio, TV and films. She teaches English, Drama and Creative Writing and works regularly as director. Anni runs her own company 'Shakespeare Link,' taking Shakespeare workshops to schools and colleges. She has written several workbooks on Shakespeare, now used in many schools. Her poem 'Empty Cradle' is published in the anthology *Secret and Silent Tears*. Anni is currently writing a novel called *Breaking The Maafa Chain*.

Layn Feldman lives in Suffolk, having emigrated from Golders Green over eleven years ago. Now retired, she appears to spend her time seeking out cafes that serve the best cappuccinos, thinking about gardening, complaining about stuff, complying with the mum contract by worrying about her three grown up kids, caring for her two cats Tigger and Roo (the daughter chose the names), taking her dog Dylan (after Bob) for walks, knitting, shouting at the radio and the telly, chatting to friends, sleeping and writing short stories.

Wendy Gill lives in Hertfordshire with her partner, children and two dachshunds. Several years ago, she gave up a successful career in business and commerce to pursue her love of writing. She has an MA in Creative Writing from Middlesex University. Her first short story 'Moving Mike' was published in the anthology *Stations* in 2012 by Arachne Press. She has also written a libretto for a contemporary London-based musical and is currently working on a collection of short stories for women, entitled *The Female Condition*.

Belona Greenwood is a former journalist who escaped to Norwich where she did an MA in Scriptwriting at the University of East Anglia. She has won an Escalator award for creative non-fiction, is a winner of the Decibel Penguin prize for life-writing and writes plays for adults and children. She is founder and co-organiser of Words And Women.

Caroline Jackson is a freelance writer who lives in Cambridge with her husband and two teenage children. She studied English at university before a brief, and not long lamented, career as a lawyer. Currently writing a novel set in Ireland, she is easily distracted by blogging as Oxonian in Cambridge, reviewing books for various magazines and the urge to write short stories.

Alice Kent was born in Oxford. She studied Philosophy at the University of Birmingham, followed by an MA in European Journalism at Cardiff. She is currently working on a collection of essays inspired by ten years of working in marketing – *Kind Regards* – is a personal ode to the literary heroes of office life including Pessoa, Gogol and Kafka. She is also working on an essay about collective memory, comparing Ishiguro and Sebald, and a novel based around mass hysteria. She works at Norwich University of the Arts and lives in Norwich.

C.G. Menon grew up in Australia and has lived in the UK for five years. She's currently based in Cambridge. She studied mathematics at the Australian National University and has attended creative writing courses at City University in London. Catherine has previously been published in Everyday Fiction, and has work upcoming in a Stupefying Stories anthology.

Lily Meyer grew up in Washington, DC. She recently graduated from Brown University in Providence, Rhode Island and is a Master's student in Creative Writing at the University of East Anglia.

Patricia Mullin graduated from Central/St Martins and became a textile designer for Liberty & Co London. Later, as an illustrator, her work featured in women's magazines, publishing and industry publications. In 2007 Patricia graduated from the MA Writing the Visual at Norwich University for the Arts. In 2009 Patricia was shortlisted for an Arts Council Escalator Award. Anthology publications include short stories Archie and the Dragon, The Camera Lies and Terrafrimerites. Her 2005 novel *Gene Genie* was republished as an e–book in 2012. Patricia has led site-specific writing courses at the Julian Shrine, Norwich Cathedral and most recently at the Sainsbury Centre for the Visual Arts. She is an associate lecturer at the University of East Anglia. Currently she is revising two novels that have been languishing in a drawer, also putting the finishing touches to her recent novel *Casting Shadows*.

Karen O'Connor has been writing fiction on and off for fifteen years and has previously had four short stories published or shortlisted in competitions. These include: A Week Off If You Sell the Lot, 'Take a Break's Fiction Feast', Shooting Stars, 'Writers News' (2nd prize winner in their writing competition), My Final Blog, 'Words With Jam' (awarded second place in their short story competition) and Dead Perfect, 'Writers News' (shortlisted in their 1,000 word writing competition). She is currently writing book five of a series of young adult novels.

Judith Omasete is originally from Kenya, where she worked with International Non Governmental Organizations, dealing with agricultural development, healthcare, education, child welfare, micro enterprises, tourism, conservation and land tenure. Now Judith lives in Norfolk with her family and has worked as a high school teaching assistant for 4 years. She has run workshops in schools for Norfolk Education Action for Development (NEAD) and is currently pursuing further education.

Bridget Read is studying for the MA Biography and Creative Non-fiction at UEA. Before coming to Norwich in September 2013, she worked for New York and Guernica magazines, and was living in Brooklyn, New York. She graduated from Wesleyan University in Middletown, Connecticut in 2012 and grew up in Los Angeles and Washington, D.C.

Dani Redd grew up in the South West of England, studied English Literature at Queen Mary's University, and is currently a student on the MA Creative Writing Course at Norwich's UEA. Dani has been shortlisted and placed in several short fiction competitions and most recently was longlisted for The Lightship Short Story Prize. She is currently working on her first novel, which is set on a fictional island within the arctic circle.

Elizabeth Reed is currently working on her first novel, an historical thriller set in 6th Century BC Delphi. Her previous writing has included educational and marketing materials, news articles, pop songs and – since attending two creative writing courses in the past year – short fiction. What seems like a long, long time ago she received a first class BA degree in English and Drama from Loughborough University and then studied for an MA in English and American Literature and Film in New York. After 20 years of living in London she returned to Norwich where she was born and raised and now divides her time between there and Gran Canaria where she occasionally works as a singer.

Bethany Settle has an MA in Creative Writing: Prose from the University of East Anglia. She remained in Norwich, where she works at a library. Reading, writing and nature are her top three best things. She is writer-in-residence at the Rumsey Wells pub in Norwich, and is currently writing a novel that explores grief and loss.

Kim Sherwood tours with literary salons Elbow Room and The Book Club Boutique, and has published short stories and poetry. She completed the BA in Literature with Creative Writing at UEA in 2011, receiving the Jarrold Prize for most outstanding performance. She continued on to the Prose Fiction MA, and is now a fellowship student on the Creative and Critical Writing PhD. Kim writes in Norwich, London, Devon, and the quiet coach. She is writing her first novel.

Nedra Westwater, a Midwestern American by birth, has a BA in English literature from the University of Wisconsin. She travelled to Brazil as a Fulbright Scholar in 1960, where she met and married the Scottish designer Norman Westwater. In 1966 she, her husband and small son moved from Rio to Lavenham, Suffolk. She has since lived in London, Portugal and Santa Fe, where she was a founder-member of PEN New Mexico. Nedra's writing, often illustrated with her own photographs, has been published in journals in England, Portugal, the United States and other countries. She has lived in Norwich since 2003 and received an Escalator Literature

2006 Special Commendation for a chapter of her memoir about Salvador, Bahia – an ongoing work.

Rowan Whiteside was born in Durban, South Africa but has spent most of her life in the fine city of Norwich. She works as Marketing Assistant for Writers' Centre Norwich and as a bookseller for Waterstones, where she was formerly the manager of the fiction department. Rowan studied English and American Literature at the University of East Anglia, where she snuck onto as many creative writing classes as possible and read a lot of books from the Classics section. Her writing has been published online on various sites and 'zines. She can be found on Twitter @DilysTolfree.

Lois Williams grew up along the Wash coast and travelled widely, teaching English in university and community writing programmes in the US. Her poems and essays have appeared in many venues, including Verse Daily, New England Review, Antiphon, and Granta. She is busy completing a book of stories, *The Invention of Home*, from which "The House of Provisions" was awarded a notable essay listing in Best American Essays 2009. She lives in Norfolk, working as a freelance writer and visual artist, and volunteering with ecology and habitat restoration projects.

Lightning Source UK Ltd.
Milton Keynes UK
UKOW03f2127310314

229187UK00005B/391/P